Dream Mountain

THE MYSTERIOUS LEDGE

BY
LOREN HALLORAN

ILLUSTRATED BY FARIA AHSAN

Dream Mountain
Copyright © 2021 by Loren Halloran

ISBN
978-1-954932-88-3 (Paperback)
978-1-954932-87-6 (eBook)

Table of Contents

This book is dedicated to my Grandson Jackson, as well as to my four wonderful children, Megan, Rylie, Jordyn and Isaiah. I pray you develop the passion to write. Aspire to inspire.

About the Author

Loren Halloran lives and writes from his home in Powell River, on the Sunshine Coast of south western British Columbia. Canada. Loren's passion for writing includes many recorded songs, two novels called The Mysterious Ledge and Dream Mountain, a children's book called Gunky Life, and an adult collection of inter-relational poetry pieces called Scrawl on the Garden Wall. When not writing Loren can be found riding his Harley-Davidson along Powell River's ocean highway, or playing his beloved keyboards.

ONE

Forever Friends

Twenty years had passed since Georgy dreamed about climbing the mountain and standing on the ledge. The dream had been surreal and now as a man in his early thirties, he found something nudging him to write about it.

Georgy had gone to university and had become a Conservation Officer. That had always been what he'd wanted to be. He knew that in his heart he had a story to tell and so he felt the time was right to begin. It might take a while but he was set on a name for the book. It would be called Dream Mountain.

One Sunday morning in August, as Georgy was attending church, he noticed a beautiful woman who he didn't recognize, sitting alone in a pew. She seemed to be about his age. Georgy, being the gentleman that he is, introduced himself and welcomed her to church. He asked if he could sit down. The lady smiled and motioned for him to have a seat beside her.

"Anna is my name and I'm here visiting this beautiful area for the next number of days" she said. "I'm from New York and had heard about the Vancouver Island lifestyle. I had wanted to experience it for myself so took some vacation days to come here. "Why Lake Cowichan" Georgy asked. "I saw the beautiful Cowichan sweaters on the internet and wanted to see where they were made so I rented a car and came here. They are made here, right Georgy, in Lake Cowichan?" She asked. "Not quite, but close to us in Duncan" he assured her.

After the service, Georgy offered to take Anna out for a drive and then lunch in Duncan. This way she could get an idea of some of the sights around the area and would be taken right to the places that offered the crafts she was wanting to see.

"Thanks Georgy, that's very kind of you to offer. I'd love to go with you. I'm sure you'd be an amazing tour guide." "Okay, brace yourself because I know just the spot to take you for lunch," Georgy said. "We'll stop to get some coffee to go and then take the thirty-minute drive to Duncan." "This sounds perfect. I'd love a cup of coffee," she said.

Georgy and Anna drove over to a coffee shop and ordered some coffee to go then set out for the drive to Duncan. Anna told him that she'd arrived the day before but because of her flight, renting the car and making the drive from Victoria to Duncan, she was only wanting to rest, so didn't get around town to see anything except for the church. "I'm so happy that I didn't skip church today then," Georgy snickered. "You'd have been gone by next Sunday," he said.

They made their way past the dispersed small farms on the way to Duncan. Anna commented on how rural the living must be and asked how self reliant the families were. "All of these folks have big gardens, some horses, cows and chickens. They each have a small field for hay to feed the horses and a few acres of field for the cows to graze on. Everyone has a wood stove. They keep themselves in meat by butchering for a side of beef, and they generally sell the other side of beef to raise cash. You'll see signs along their driveways for eggs they are selling as they have way too many eggs to eat. They select meat chickens for eating and leave the egg laying chickens to produce the eggs. They live as frugally as possible but the work is demanding. The lifestyle is a healthy one," Georgy said. "Don't forget the wood that is needed to heat the home. It gets pretty cold in the winter season so they must keep the wood up all year round."

Georgy pulled into Duncan and Anna immediately noticed a tall totem pole standing beside the recreation complex. "That looks fantastic Georgy," she commented. "They are everywhere Anna," Georgy replied as he pulled into the Native Cultural Centre. Anna was amazed to see many more totems and carved wooden pieces that greeted them as they entered the parking lot.

The café was located inside the Centre which was situated beside a river. Native masks and hand-woven baskets lined the walls creating many conversation pieces. The servers were wearing native designs printed on the dress shirts they were wearing. The fashion wear looked gorgeous. Anna was given a menu that boasted aboriginal dishes. Georgy explained the menu to Anna who couldn't wait to taste it.

Anna selected a sockeye salmon dish with traditional bannock and berries. Georgy had moose stew with fry bread and a berry pie for dessert. "This food was absolutely delightful and the atmosphere stunning," Anna said. "The servers were so friendly and dressed up in such a sharp and classy way too."

After lunch they made their way over to the shops in town that carried aboriginal pieces. Anna was thrilled with the arrangement of hand-woven baskets, masks, articles of clothing wood carvings and jewellery. The paintings were done in primary colours and looked outstanding. Anna made her way over to the jewellery showcase and stared at the craftsmanship displayed on the gold and silver bracelets. There were rings, bangles and earrings that stole her heart.

"Look over here Anna. I think this is what you really wanted to see," Georgy said. When Anna got to Georgy he was in another small room. It was loaded with Cowichan sweaters, toques, gloves and leather moccasins. There was so much to take in. Dream catchers dangled above them. The deer-hide coats with colourful beads embroidered on them looked spectacular too. Small totems and hand painted drums with eagle feathers were set against another wall in the room. Anna picked out a scarf with a striking design on it as they were about to leave the Gallery. "That was wicked!" she said. "We need to come back very soon."

They decided to park and stroll the downtown area. There was a totem pole walkabout with yellow painted footprints on the sidewalk that would lead you to the next totem. It was such a spectacle to see the colour and the intricate etching that went into carving the characters on the totems. Each totem had a brass plaque that explained its origin and significance. It also told of the date it was erected.

After about an hour of looking they decided to head back to Lake Cowichan. Georgy promised Anna that he would take her to the museum and show her around the outskirts of the city the next day. Anna was so happy. She commented on how friendly the people were that she passed by on the sidewalk. She said it wasn't like that back home.

Anna was staying in a Bed and Breakfast. When they got to her place Georgy asked if he could take her out for a glass of wine after dinner. "Maybe we should just go out to get dinner," Anna said. "That way we can reflect on today and better plan our day tomorrow." Georgy couldn't refuse the offer. "Only if you let me cook dinner for you tomorrow evening Anna," Georgy replied. They looked into each other's eyes and then gave each other a hug. "I really enjoyed today Georgy. I can't wait to learn more about this lifestyle here," Anna said. "See you in an hour," Georgy said.

Georgy left feeling excited that he'd found a new friend in Anna. He went home and began to clean up the house. He wanted to make a good impression on Anna. Georgy had a quick shower and in no time, he was on his way to pick up Anna. Georgy got there and she was ready to go. Georgy asked Anna what she'd like to eat and she suggested Chinese food. Georgy loved Chinese food too. They made their way back to Duncan as there were no Chinese food restaurants in Lake Cowichan.

Georgy and Anna talked all the way to Duncan. Anna was fascinated with the two towns and asked Georgy about the cities and towns in the rest of the province. She told Georgy she had looked up other communities but said she really had wanted to be near the ocean. After Georgy explained some of the northern cities to her, she admitted that she had already decided on Vancouver Island, where they were, as there is a lot less winter and snow by the ocean. She told Georgy that she'd pretty well made up her mind that she wanted to live out the rest of her life here where they were. Georgy was elated. "There's much to do then," Georgy said. "Especially if we only have under a week to explore together."

When they were finished eating dinner Georgy took Anna for a stroll by the ocean. He'd brought along a poncho to keep her warm. "I feel like I'm in heaven," Anna said. Georgy pointed out a pod of about 15 sea lions as they swam buy in single file and barking noisily. "They're so loud Georgy," Anna shouted. At that very moment two eagles appeared on the scene. They seemed to be fighting as they had locked talons in mid flight. "One of the eagles has something to eat in his talons and the other one is trying to pry it loose." It surely was a sight to see.

Georgy told Anna he would show her some of the beaches after the museum tomorrow. He said that they needed to get back to

Lake Cowichan as there would be deer and elk on the highway and it was getting dark out. Sure enough, Georgy spotted some yellowy-green eyes on the side of the road. "Look Anna, over there. There's a bunch of elk just waiting to walk up onto the road. They are the size of horses. People that hit the elk are usually injured and their cars severely damaged. If it were deer, they would dart across the road following each other and it wouldn't allow you to stop in time, Georgy said. "That certainly is scary. I'll watch for more eyes," Anna said.

When they got home, Anna told Georgy that she was so thankful for all that they did and saw while in Duncan, and for keeping her safe on their drive back home. When Anna got out of the car, she told Georgy that she couldn't wait until tomorrow. "I can't wait either Anna. I don't want this to ever end," Georgy said. They exchanged phone numbers and said they'd talk in the morning.

Anna gave Georgy a hug through the window. "Thank you for taking time off your work schedule to show me around," Anna said. "It's my pleasure. I have a lot of vacation days to use up." Georgy said laughing. "Sleep well Anna." "Sweet dreams Georgy and thanks again for the yummy dinner." Anna said.

Georgy went home to his house to collect his thoughts. He felt so happy spending the time with Anna. As he got ready for bed, he couldn't stop thinking of how fortunate he was in having Anna for a friend. She and Georgy really seemed to be getting along. He got into bed and was now set to have a wonderful sleep.

Early the next morning Georgy awoke to hear someone knocking loudly on his front door. It was his friend Jason Miller. Georgy had forgotten he'd be there first thing Monday morning to discuss some landscaping ideas in the hopes of upgrading the appearance of his property.

Together they planned out a massive garden, a large area for wild flowers, places for planter boxes to be filled with colourful pansies and an underground watering system that would take everything, including the lawn into account. Jason mentioned that he had a small wooden bridge that would allow people to cross the creek that ran across Georgy's property. He also agreed to create a small pond using a big back-ho, and would plant a shady maple tree beside the pond for shade later when the tree got bigger.

Georgy felt really good by the changes that would be made. He couldn't help but think that Anna would be delighted to learn of his plans. Georgy said goodbye to Jason and immediately called Anna on the phone. Anna had slept well, as Georgy had hoped she would. She had already showered and had her continental breakfast, courtesy of the Bed and Breakfast. Georgy told her he would shower and pick her up in thirty minutes.

When Georgy got there Anna was standing outside waiting. She had a big grin on her face. "I wanted to tell you that I'm excited for this day and grateful for you being there for me "Anna said. "I'm excited to be able to be spending another day with you too Anna," Georgy replied. "I'd like to show you where I live before heading into Duncan. I've just met with a landscaping friend and would like to share the proposed changes with you, if you don't mind." "I'd like to see where you live Georgy," Anna retorted.

As Georgy pulled into his driveway Anna gasped. "You own all of this Georgy?" "Yes, I bought it from my parents. It was their hobby farm. This is where I grew up. We had a few cows, horses, and a lot of chickens. I still keep some egg laying chickens but the other animals were sold off when I was attending university. My parents had decided that there was too much upkeep with the hobby farm and began to try to downsize. I helped my parents move into town when I finished university and began to take over the place, eventually buying it from them." It's absolutely gorgeous," Anna said.

Georgy told Anna of all the proposed changes to the property. "Oh my, will this ever be beautiful" Anna exclaimed. "How big is the property Georgy?" "I ended up keeping three acres, which is enough for what I wanted. The hay fields weren't needed anymore so I sold them off. This size enables me to have a big garden, larger than the one my parents had," Georgy said.

Georgy's friend Jason had done well with his business. He'd studied horticulture and landscaping in university and had become well known throughout the Cowichan Valley with his new business. Jason's parents had sold the General Store and were living in the same complex as Georgy's parents. The new owners had renovated the store and had added a soda bar, milkshake and ice cream station and had turned it into a really popular place to frequent. They kept the name since it had been so well known over the years.

Anna was thrilled for Georgy and told him so. "Georgy, what would you think of putting a porch swing beside the pond? I think it might be nice to sit and look over the property," Anna hinted. "Are you telling me that you would want to be sitting with me in this porch swing?" Georgy asked.

"I know it's only been a few days but I feel that I want to spend the rest of my life here. What would you say to me going back home, quitting my job, and putting in my notice at my apartment?" Anna asked. "I'd be absolutely thrilled!" Georgy replied. "Do you feel it's too soon Georgy?" Anna asked. "One day at a time. I'd love for you to move here Anna but wherever would you live?" Georgy laughed. "I guess if you'd let me stay in the wood shed I might be able to make a go of it", Anna replied. "Things happen for a reason. The minute I first laid eyes on you in church I felt something for you Anna," Georgy confided. "God is good. He brought you all the way here and we were able to meet each other. Tell me that's not meant to be," Georgy said. "I'm pretty sure you wouldn't have to stay in the wood shed," Georgy laughed.

It was in that moment Georgy and Anna looked into each other's eyes and hugged each other. And it was then they shared their first kiss.

Georgy mentioned that they should go to Duncan, to the museum. Anna was ready. When they got there Georgy found that the museum wasn't open yet so he took her to a special place called the Kinsol Trestle, a Historical Landmark which is one of the tallest free-standing and most spectacular timber rail structures in the world.

When they got there Anna was shocked at the enormous size and beauty of the trestle. The trestle stands 44 meters above the salmon bearing Koksilah River and is 187 meters in length. Georgy and Anna walked hand in hand across the trestle and back. The river was a long way down.

After their walk they made their way back to the museum. It was a small place but was loaded with all sorts of really cool stuff. There were old tools, bowls, hand made baskets, various wood carvings and many leather pieces of clothing. There was even a birch bark canoe and hand painted paddle that lined the back wall. Anna was fascinated by all that she saw there.

Soon it was time for lunch. Georgy took Anna to a nearby organic bakery and café for some alternative food and drink.

As they waited for their orders, Anna began talking about her background. She had graduated from music collage In New York and had been working as a singer in a radio station studio doing jingles for their client's radio commercials. She worked a lot of evenings and she'd become tired over the past few years. Life in the big city had also begun to take a toll on her. This led her to begin researching life on the west coast of Vancouver Island and wanted to see first hand, what it would be like to visit for a week. This is what got her to Lake Cowichan. She'd booked a week off and flew to Victoria, British Columbia's capital city, located on the west coast of Vancouver Island. From there she rented a car and had driven to Lake Cowichan.

Georgy and Anna had begun to be smitten with each other. Anna stayed the remainder of her time with Georgy. She prepared meals for him so he could go back to work and come home to a hot meal, something Georgy hadn't had since leaving home years ago. Anna was an amazing cook and she also loved to bake.

Sunday finally came around and this time, instead of going to church, Georgy offered to drive Anna to the airport in Victoria. She had returned her rental car after she met Georgy, so she needed him to get her to the airport, which Georgy wanted to do anyway. Her vacation time was over and she needed to get back home to begin winding down on her job etc. When they got there, Georgy helped Anna get her place in line and gave her a big, long hug. As they kissed each other goodbye, Georgy reminded her that they were just a phone call away from each other and they shared the same purpose which was to get back together as soon as possible. Anna said goodbye and said she'd keep in touch with Georgy to let him know how things were working out. She then made her way into the waiting area.

Georgy left the airport. His head was spinning with everything he wanted to get done in preparation for Anna's return. He also realized that Anna had a lot to get done before coming back to him too, so he agreed in his own mind to do the very best he could at one day at a time and hope for the best.

Anna phoned to say she'd put her notice in to leave her apartment, with her landlord and her notice to quit work with her boss. Things were beginning to happen.

TWO

Home Face Lift

Georgy kept himself busy at home after work and on days off. Jason was in full swing working on Georgy's homestead project. Georgy decided to paint his home since he couldn't help with the landscaping. It took all month to complete but when it was done it looked like new. He knew Anna would like it too. He decided to buy some new cozy living room furniture and some new pots and pans. He even bought a hanging displayer for the pots and pans to save cupboard space. He tried to think about what Anna would like when she moved in. He asked Jason's wife and she said that if she liked to bake, he must have things like a good mix master and other kitchen appliances that included a great working stove. Georgy decided to upgrade his old fridge and stove for new stainless-steel ones.

For the bedroom he bought a new bedroom suite. Dressers, a vanity and mirror, a new bed with both regular and flannel sheets and pillow cases. New towels and facecloths adorned the bathroom and ensuite. Soon enough Georgy felt that Anna would be well taken care of.

Anna would be arriving in another two weeks. Georgy was getting excited. He and Anna talked every other day on the phone but he had kept the painting of the house and the home purchases a secret because he really wanted her to be surprised when she got there.

Well, the day finally came. Georgy set off for Victoria to pick up Anna. He brought his work pick up with a covered canopy, expecting that Anna would have a lot of luggage. Georgy entered the terminal with flowers in hand. He waited patiently for Anna to arrive. A few minutes later Anna arrived, her face beaming with joy. They embraced and nearly squashed the flowers. "Finally!" Georgy exclaimed. "What a whirlwind the last month and a half has been," Anna answered. "I've got a lot of luggage Georgy. I hope you don't mind. I sold and gave away so much stuff just to get here. "I brought a pick up with a canopy just in case," he said. They loaded up the luggage and put it into the truck. "You're here safe and sound and that's what matters," Georgy said.

"Has this really happened Georgy?" Anna asked in disbelief. "Oh yes it has and the best is yet to come," he hinted. "You just wait until we get home. You won't believe what Jason's team did to the property." "I can't wait to see," she replied. On the way home Georgy stopped at a drive through to get some coffee and muffins for the ride home. They gabbed the whole way home.

"What?" Anna shrieked. "You had the house painted too Georgy?" "I did it myself," Georgy replied. "I wasn't able to help Jason so I kept myself busy by painting." "It looks so beautiful,"

Anna exclaimed. "There's more Anna. Let's get your luggage inside and I will give you a tour around the place." Georgy replied. "Deal," Anna said.

It only took a minute before Anna noticed some of the changes. "Oh my God Georgy, what have you done?" Anna asked. She stared at the bedroom, checked out the bed, walked into the ensuite and noticed the new towels. "Come into the kitchen and livingroom," Georgy teased. When she walked into the kitchen, she saw the new appliances and the hanging pots and pans. "I love it!" Anna exclaimed. As she walked into the livingroom she noticed the new furniture and quickly sat on it.

"This is so comfortable Georgy. I love it. You've done so much," Anna said. She got up and gave Georgy a big hug. Let's go outside. I want to show you the changes that were made to the yard," Georgy said. Anna noticed all the planter boxes full of beautiful coloured pansies. Next, she went over to the garden area. There was so much to take in. "This is so huge!" Anna exclaimed. As they kept walking around Georgy pointed out things like the small wooden arched bridge that he placed across the creek and the wooden porch swing that was next to the pond facing the house and garden. Jason had also placed a small shady maple tree beside the pond.

Anna's face was beaming. "You remembered the porch swing Georgy" she said. "I can't wait to plant the garden. This is heaven to me. There's nothing more therapeutic than being out in the garden," Anna said. "It's so healthy doing garden work and being able to eat from the fruits of your labor," she said.

"I agree. Now I have one more surprise for you Anna. It's over here behind the house," Georgy said.

Georgy took Anna by the hand and walked her to the back side of the house. He asked Anna to close her eyes. "You can open them now Anna, "Georgy said. Anna was astonished to see that Georgy had a large cedar deck with a hot tub in it, complete with stairs and lattice panels for privacy.

"This is way over the top Georgy," Anna exclaimed. "It's nice to have someone to share it with Anna," Georgy retorted. "Let's get you unpacked so we can begin this life together," Georgy said. "Okay. Isn't it a miracle what can happen in just a few short months?" Anna asked.

So, in just a few short months, Georgy had met the girl of his dreams and was about to begin the rest of his life with her. He felt blessed by what had transpired in that very short while.

When Anna had finished unpacking, they decided to go for a short drive to a small place called Honeymoon Bay. They had a lot to talk about as Anna was a U.S. citizen and would need to apply for her Canadian citizenship. They both knew that marriage would be imminent or Anna would have to return to the U.S. They decided together to wait until August of the next year to celebrate the one-year anniversary of their meeting.

"I can't wait to plant that garden in the spring," Anna said. "There's so much to do and see Anna. I'm due to get a new 4x4 for work this January so I'll be able to take you up the mountain. I know you'll like what you see because we'll be looking down at the clouds. It's really quite spectacular," Georgy said.

It was past dinner time and Georgy suggested they buy a pizza and sit by the fire. Anna said yes, as long as she could buy some red wine to go along with it. The scene was set. After they ate, they went out to the hot tub to relax and sip their wine together. They began to talk about marriage and both agreed to having a private wedding. Georgy's one wish was that they be married in the clover field, the very place he'd had his magical dream.

Anna understood completely. She knew how much it meant to Georgy and it might prove to be significant down the road too. You see. Georgy had told Anna, in great length, about his dream, and about Will too. Will had shared a great deal with Georgy in real life, before his passing. He'd been a friend, storyteller, carver and fisherman. Will had been a very clever man and Georgy had learned a great deal from him.

"I mean the work that went into the knife, the rainstick and the walking stick," Georgy said. "And the fact that he could throw the knife. He was so very talented. Anna truly understood that Georgy was serious about recreating his dream in both story and in real life. She didn't realize how instrumental she'd be in helping to make that happen.

Not too many weeks later Anna found out she was pregnant. Both she and Georgy were ecstatic about it. Preparing for the baby would suddenly be their number one priority, although Georgy had already begun penning his dream book. He would call it Dream Mountain. He knew it would take months to write because of the vivid detail that would be involved in writing it. He didn't want to leave anything out either so he was careful to only write so much each day.

Georgy figured that it would be a good idea to start by writing pages of notes. That way he could expand on the notes later on as he'd remember more details. Little by little the manuscript began to take shape. He needed to find an illustrator to talk to about drawing the pictures he'd need. He figured about one per chapter and a front cover.

This was fun for Georgy. It was on his mind all day long. He couldn't wait to get home and add on to his story each day. He eventually found a good illustrator and began discussing the characters he'd need as pictures in his book. When Georgy had finished writing the rough draft by hand, he began to transfer it onto a Microsoft Word file. As his pictures were being drawn and sent to him, he began putting them together with the computer pages into a booklet that would enable him to see what the book would end up looking like. He kept editing and printing the pages but soon realized it would never be perfect. He finally decided that it was a finished project.

It had taken him months to complete the story but he did it, a bit at a time, every evening. "Now what will you do Georgy?" Anna asked. "I guess I need to start sending it out to some publishing companies," Georgy replied. "I'll need to see their level of interest. In the meantime, I need to start thinking of a way to get to the top of that ledge in real life," Georgy laughed.

Not too many months later Anna gave birth to a beautiful, healthy baby boy. She had the baby on Georgy's birthday. Through a little coaxing, Georgy persuaded Anna to name their son Taylor. Georgy was beside himself as he now had a son to share in his legacy of taking on that mysterious ledge when his son would get older. Georgy would take the time to teach Taylor about his dream.

THREE

Fast Forward

Taylor had turned 9. He had a few close friends that he played with. One named Bergy Bergeron had a Keystone minibike that Taylor loved getting rides on. Bergy was so lucky to own it and he was super popular amongst the other boys in school because he had the minibike. Bergy lived on the other side of the tracks, not more than a few blocks away from Taylor. Kippy and Jerry Singh were two other friends that lived up the bank behind Taylor's house. They were an East Indian family that had been neighbours to Taylor all of his life. Their mom used to give Taylor rotis, Indian flatbread when he'd come to visit. It was so yummy.

Often the four boys would ride their wagons down the hill beside Taylor's house. There was a river at the bottom of the hill, as well as a train trestle that crossed the river. The boys spent lots of time playing there. They would put pennies on the train tracks and hide in the bushes until the train went by and then squeal with delight when they found their squashed pennies.

They never had to worry about a train coming while they were on the trestle as there was a narrow walkway on either side of the tracks. There were steep dirt banks on either side of the tracks, just before the trestle. The boys liked to see how far up they could climb before sliding back down.

Georgy had asked the boys if they might be interested in working the following Saturday. He wanted to begin re-clearing the path to Will's cabin. Georgy offered to pay the boys some cash, hot dogs, pop and chips. All the boys were willing to work.

Anna was in charge of lunch. When Saturday came around the boys showed up at ten a.m., eager to get going. Georgy had rakes and a few wheelbarrows for the boys to use. He even had gloves for the boys to use and cold bottles of water in a cooler. They planned to work from 10-12 noon, have lunch and work again from 12:30-2:30.

Georgy did a bunch of branch clearing and bush cutting. The boys picked up the brush and wheeled it to an open container sitting on Georgy's property. Everybody worked hard. Georgy had a small chain saw and was really beginning to make headway.

The biggest challenge was the big tree roots that were sprawled across the pathway. Georgy didn't want to cut them as it would kill the trees so he had to be creative and put dirt around both sides of the roots. That was something he and Taylor could do another time. Georgy focused on just getting the work done that the boys could help him with as many hands make for light work. They were getting a lot done.

The boys had a great time at lunch. They were hooting and hollering and having a fun time together. Bergy promised to go get his mini bike when they were done. Georgy reminded the boys he'd be paying them for the work they were doing so they were eager to get back at it again.

By 12:30 everyone was bushed. They'd managed to clear away about half of the twigs and bush on the trail. Georgy asked the boys to put the rakes, wheelbarrows and gloves into the open container for next week. He paid them and told them to go buy some ice cream with the money.

That's exactly what Georgy did with Anna and Taylor. They got washed up and went for a drive into town. After they picked up a few groceries they headed over to Miller's General Store.

Georgy and Taylor had 2 scoop strawberry cones while Anna had a tall, cool raspberry soda. Georgy noticed that some of the original glass show cases were still being used in the store. He liked to look at pocket knives in the old cases.

Taylor loved to come into town with his folks. Just like his dad, Taylor would order an ice cream cone from Miller's Store, as soon as their shopping was done. Georgy realized that Taylor had no dog to share his cone with. "Anna, what would you think about us getting a watch dog?" Georgy asked. "I'd love it!" Anna replied. "You said that you had a dog when you were Taylor's age," she said. "Yes, he got old and died," Georgy said. "He was a black lab and was an excellent pet. So trustworthy too. I was thinking that having a dog in the trail with us might be a good thing, in terms of a bear deterrent," Georgy said. "I totally agree, Anna replied.

FOUR

My Dog Beau

Over the next few weeks Anna focused herself on finding the right dog for their home. She found a young, one year old male black lab that was located in Duncan. When Anna told Georgy, he said that was amazing, and that they'd swing by on Saturday to have a look at him.

Georgy wasted no time in telling Taylor. Taylor asked if he could name him. Georgy said that they'd have to wait and see because he probably already had a name since he was already a year old. "I can't wait until Saturday," Taylor said. "If he looks good there'll be a lot that we'll have to buy him. I'll start a list. You can help me Taylor," Georgy hinted. "Food, dog dishes and treats, "Taylor said. "A dog bed, collar, pooper scooper," Georgy said. "How about some flea shampoo and some kind of tick remover. Oh, and a long leash," Anna said. "He'll need some toys or stuffies so that he doesn't chew our shoes," Georgy said. "I think we've covered everything," Anna said. "We're going to get a dog anyway so let's just buy what we need before we get him so that we're totally ready to bring him home," Georgy said.

Saturday finally came around. Georgy, Anna and Taylor hopped in the truck and drove into Duncan. They stopped in at a large pet store to buy what they needed and then drove out to view the dog.

When they arrived, they noticed a large wire fence dog run with a black lab and a small Jack Russell dog playing together. They barked happily at the newcomers as they exited the truck. The owners welcomed them and then said that the dog's name was Beau. "We named him that because he was the most handsome dog in the litter, the people said. "That name's perfect," Taylor said to his dad. "I really like it," Georgy said. "You won't find a better dog either. He likes to come inside at night. He's a good watch dog and he loves to play. He's good with children too," the lady said.

Georgy looked at his family and asked if they should take him home. Everyone was in agreement so they paid the lady and loaded Beau into the truck. He licked Taylor all the way home. When they got home, they put the collar and leash on Beau so that Taylor could take him for a walk around the house. When everything was brought in from the truck, Georgy fed Beau.

Beau took to eating and drinking out of his dog dishes right away. He liked his new dog bed too. Georgy put it near the fireplace. They decided that Beau should sleep in Taylor's room until he was comfortable being in the living room by himself. Beau ended up being Anna's responsibility since Georgy was at work and Taylor was at school each day. At first, they kept Beau on a leash when he went out for a walk but soon enough, they let him go off leash because he never ran away. When Taylor would get home from school they'd run around the property. Beau was just interested in playing. He wasn't allowed in the garden area. Georgy was not wanting to have to build a fence so they needed to train him to stay away from the area.

Georgy allowed them to play over in the clover field, the same place he and his dog Ben used to play at. Kippy and Jerry would often come to play fetch with Beau after school too. They didn't have any pets of their own so this was a lot of fun for them as well. Bergy would show up with his mini bike and try to get Beau to catch him. Bergy wouldn't let anyone ride his bike but he was awesome at giving everybody rides. Beau certainly got his exercise running after Bergy and playing fetch with the other boys.

Soon they'd have to be heading home for dinner. Beau would be thirsty so Taylor would often turn on the outside tap and let Beau try to lap up water from the hose. He loved resting in his dog bed after his play time. He was turning out to be a really good fit for the family.

Anna had begun to sing on the praise team at church. The worship leader had talked with Anna about her joining and knew of her capability. Anna's voice was like liquid gold. She often sang solos and it wasn't too long before word got out that she'd been a professional singer.

Anna began to get calls to sing in bands, and then one person, who lived in Vancouver, who was visiting one weekend asked if she'd consider doing part time singing in the studio there. That was what she used to do. She talked with her family about it and agreed to come over twice a month on Saturdays, to sing in the studio.

Georgy was both pleased and surprised by Anna's singing voice. He encouraged Anna to be the very best she could be and Anna loved the support he gave her. She loved Georgy and was definitely loving her life.

As the next few months went by, they found themselves smack dab in the middle of winter. It was December and there was snow on the mountains, and all around the valley. They'd get light snowfalls but nothing that would stick around for days at a time. Black ice was more of a problem on the main highway. When it did snow, Georgy would let the kids hang on to the back bumper and he'd take them for rides, letting them skid around in the snow. What fun it was.

One morning Georgy asked Anna if she'd like to go up the mountain with him in the company 4x4. She said sure so they took off up a logging road. After a few miles they began the ascent up the mountain. The road was very narrow up to the top. Georgy's truck was decked out with front and back winches, extra driving lights, including fog lights and big snow tires with chains. It came equipped with a C.B. radio and antenna which allowed him to radio the other logging truck drivers who might be in the area. The two-way radio was a must as the oncoming drivers would not be able to stop in time if they met you suddenly, as they came down the mountain side, fully loaded.

Georgy told Anna that if that ever happened, drivers of other vehicles would have to hit the ditch or risk being injured or even killed as the road was only wide enough for one vehicle and that the logging trucks had the right of way. Georgy called out over the radio every couple of minutes so as to let the truckers know where on the road he was. Small sign posts were placed along the roadside that were location markers telling you what mile you were at so you could let the logging truck drivers know. You wouldn't want to chance being hit by a truck carrying a full load of logs.

A short time later they reached the mountain top. They got out and walked over to the edge to look down the mountain side. They were looking down on the clouds. It was so amazing to see. "I've never seen anything quite like this before, except for being in an airplane," Anna said. "That's low cloud cover," Georgy said. "We are pretty high up here though," Georgy added. At that moment they heard and saw a brown flash move quickly a short distance away. As they moved back toward the truck, they noticed a cougar that was stalking a deer. "That's pretty normal for up her. Let's make our way back down the mountain side Anna," Georgy said.

As they got back into the truck, they watched the deer run off. The cougar stayed put and only walked away when Georgy drove past it. The ride down the mountain side was scary for Anna. The road was so narrow that if they were to meet another vehicle, someone would have to back up. It would be horrible to do as pullouts were few and far between on the mountain.

Georgy got down safely without a problem. Anna was happy to not to ever go again anytime soon. "What if we slipped and went over the edge Georgy?" Anna asked. "That's why we have airbags Anna," Georgy laughed. "Don't worry, I'm a very careful driver, "Georgy said.

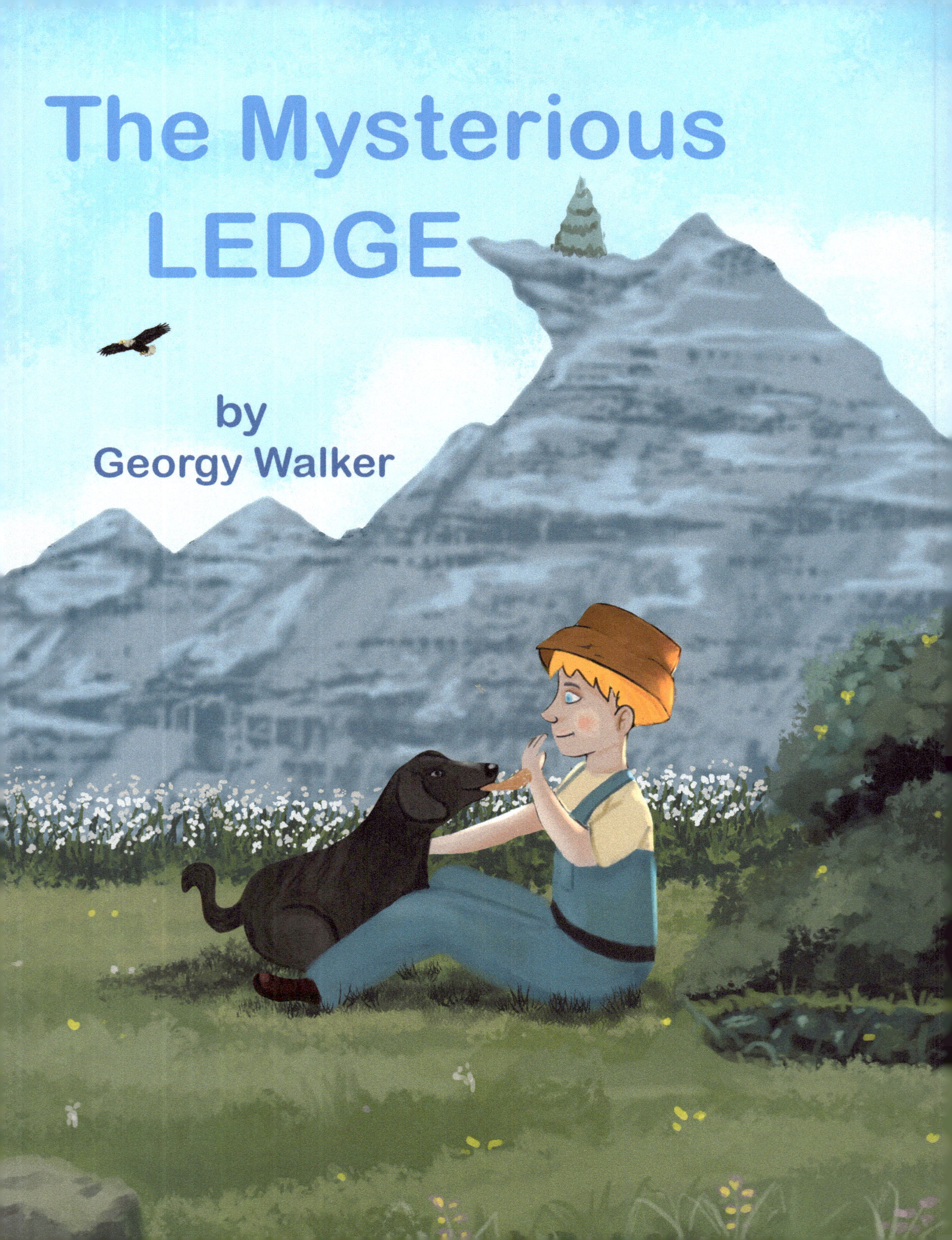

The Mysterious
LEDGE
by
Georgy Walker

FIVE

Published at Last

Georgy was determined to get his book published. He sent his manuscript to a large publishing company in the States. About a week after they received it, they contacted Georgy as they were interested in his book. So, for the next few months, Georgy kept in touch with the publishing company and together, pieced his manuscript and pictures into a beautiful novel. He was so pleased. He let the local newspapers know to get the word out. He received some personal copies and couldn't wait to see what kind of interest there might be in the Cowichan Valley.

Georgy approached the local library and some book stores in Duncan to see if they might support him. To his surprise they both featured local authors and said they'd be happy to take on his books. He'd done his best at getting the word out. He mentioned in a newspaper article that the books were available in both places.

Anna was excited that her husband had become a published author. She reminded Georgy that he was going to bring attention to the mountain with his book so he'd better get started on getting something happening on the mountain. "Don't worry Anna. I've got a plan. Once winter is over, I'll get the boys out to help me.

There'll be another election this year for city councillors. I've been hinted at to think about running this year," Georgy said. "I just know how important it is to you Georgy, especially now that the book is out," Anna said. "For now, let's put some thought into planning what we're going to plant in the garden," Georgy said.

March roared in like a lion. Georgy and Anna were buying the seed that they'd need for the garden. They'd decided on a section each for corn, potatoes, lettuce, cabbage, carrots and squash. Then beets, peppers, radishes, tomatoes and peas. This was going to yield way more than their family could eat but Georgy had a plan. He'd get a roadside stand made and sell bags of mixed vegetables and fresh cut wild flowers for cheap. He expected that it would catch on going into summer. He'd always have Taylor hanging around home to work the stand.

Anna had found her own paradise. She was married to a wonderful, giving man, had an amazing son, a dog and a beautiful home with a massive garden. She worked just enough with the studio to be pleased that her gift of singing could still be utilized. Anna had just heard that there was a successful business man from Duncan that owned some acreage in the Lake town who was planning to create an annual five-day country music festival that would be called Sunfest. It would be held on the Lake town acreage and would feature many local and out of town bands, as well as Headliners from Nashville. It was going to be huge and would take place during the August long weekend.

The business owner phoned Anna and asked her if she might be interested in meeting with him to discuss the venture. Anna was very excited for the opportunity. "You'll fit right in," Georgy kidded. The business man was well known and if anybody could pull this off, he could.

Anna attended the meeting and decided this would be an opportunity to help promote musicians and bands from the west coast of Vancouver Island, as well as from Vancouver and other cities in the province.

"Looks like I'll have to exclude you from the trail clearing and mountain road prepping this summer Anna," Georgy said. "They won't be ready this year but the land has been cleared and they will begin the construction of the stages now," Anna said. "There's so much to do and if the Headliners aren't booked a year in advance, they will be booked to perform elsewhere," Anna exclaimed with a worried look on her face.

It was in that moment that Georgy knew that he'd be alone in his efforts to make getting to the top of that mountain a reality. He wanted Anna to be the very best she could be and she had encouraged Georgy to follow his dream. She knew that there was nothing that could stop him from achieving his goal.

Since the garden had been planted, Georgy could now finish clearing the path that led to Will's cabin. Taylor and his friends continued to help Georgy every Saturday and Georgy never forgot to reward them for their hard work. Beau always had the time of his life running up and down the trail. Finally, after a few short weekends the trail had been cleared. They'd finally made it to Will's cabin.

Georgy found himself staring at the white cross that marked the spot where Will had been laid to rest. Will's family had told Georgy that it was his wish to be buried beside his cabin which was so dear to him. They had honoured his wish. Georgy focused on the words printed on the cross. They read Chief, teacher, and friend to all. It brought a smile to Georgy's face.

A thought suddenly occurred to Georgy. He would set up a wooden bench facing Will's gravesite. It would be a nice place to rest for a few minutes after walking the trail. Will's cabin had been cleaned out after his passing. It was deemed to be too old to fix up and Will's family wanted to leave it as it was so that Will and his cabin could rest in peace together.

Georgy got hold of Will's family to ask permission to have a bench placed on the property. They were more than happy to let this happen. They liked the idea of having it there for anyone to sit and reflect for a bit.

Georgy had a bench made and situated it where he wanted it to be, at the start of the pathway, facing Will's grave. Will's family came over to touch up the lawn every couple of weeks. They kept the grounds neat and made sure the white cross was freshly painted every year.

The time came where Georgy had the opportunity to run for a position in City Hall. He'd considered running over the past year and felt strongly about becoming a city councillor. As luck would have it, he was successfully voted in.

Georgy's duties would include him considering the well being and interests of the municipality and its community, and to contribute to the development and evaluation of municipal policies and programs, respecting its services and other activities.

Now Georgy could start focusing on getting a road built up the mountain. It would take a while but as time went by, Georgy was able to get approval to have a road and viewpoint built up on the ledge. It would make for an amazing view overlooking the town and surrounding area.

Georgy was made aware of an old forestry access road that hadn't been used in decades. Georgy began to work with surveyors and with the help of some ATVs, began measuring the slope involved as they made their way up the mountain side. Although it was only about a half a mile to the top, hairpin turns would be needed due to the steep grades in getting up and coming down the mountain.

Georgy's plan was for a single lane of traffic on both sides of the road and then a parking lot at the top. There would be a fenced area around the lookout right at the ledge. He envisioned a stationary, metal binocular unit in place that would allow folks to get a good look down below and across the valley to the mountains on the other side of the valley.

In Georgy's mind, he could see the beauty of providing this landmark to the city. The possibilities were endless down the road as there would be room for small tables and chairs, with umbrellas and the odd coffee or ice cream vendor in the summer. The view would be spectacular and who knows, maybe a few hiking trails could be set in place for people to enjoy a hike along the other parts of the mountain.

Georgy also envisioned some live music and or art up on the ledge. He felt strong that he could eventually make this all happen for his community. It would be a long process so it would have to be one step at a time. For now, it would be getting the road done first.

SIX

Trail Prank

Taylor talked Bergy into bringing his minibike into the trail. What fun it was scooting up and down the trail with Beau in hot pursuit. One Saturday, Kippy and Jerry went to see if Taylor could play. Anna told the boys that Bergy had been by and that they were playing in the trail on the minibike.

The boys said thanks and then Kippy suddenly had an idea. He and Jerry ran back to their house and grabbed a black bearskin rug, complete with the head on it. Kippy's plan was to hide in it and lunge toward the boys as they got close to him in the trail. He told Jerry to get some ketchup to smear on him to make it look like the bear got him. Jerry would lay on the trail where Bergy couldn't miss him. Kippy would growl and lunge at the boys on the minibike as they were stopped.

This was going to be good. They could hear the minibike further up the trail. They'd be down in a few minutes so the boys got into position. Sure enough, the boys showed up. Bergy stopped the bike to see what the big lump blocking the trail was.

"Taylor, that's Jerry. He's bleeding," Bergy shrieked. "Let's help him," Taylor shouted. At that very second, Kippy, wearing the bearskin rug, jumped out from behind the bushes growling out loud. Both boys screamed and ran for their lives. Beau charged at the bearskin but Kippy was able to toss it to one side, just in the nick of time. Kippy and Jerry were beside themselves in laughter. They shouted out to Bergy and Taylor who had stopped running and were hiding behind trees looking to see if the bear was attacking Jerry.

The boys heard Kippy and Jerry laughing. They raced back to the scene of the crime. "Holy crap you scared us. You guys got us good," Bergy laughed. "That bearskin is the real thing," Taylor said, out of breath. Beau was trying to lick the ketchup off of Jerry's face as Jerry wrestled with Beau. "That was priceless. Good thing I was able to throw the rug before Beau could tear it apart. My parents would have killed me," Kippy said. "I'm just glad I didn't crash my minibike. I thought you were dead Jerry," Bergy said. "When I heard the growling, I thought for sure you'd been attacked by a bear, and then when Kippy came out of the bushes like that, I thought we were all going to be eaten," Bergy said.

At that moment they heard a loud rustling sound in the bushes nearby to where they were standing. It even spooked Beau. The boys took off running. Kippy grabbed the rug and Bergy and Taylor shouted for the guys to get out of the way, so that Bergy could get past them on his minibike. Beau followed in hot pursuit. Taylor happened to look back and saw a large deer jump out of the bushes. "Deer!" Georgy shouted. The boys stopped to discuss what had just happened.

"That's about enough scary stuff to last for the next month" Taylor said. "Let's get out of these woods and play under the trestle." Bergy said. "I'll take the rug home and Jerry can wash the ketchup off his face. We'll see you over there," Kippy said. "And I'll take my bike home and be right over too," Bergy said. "Okay, see you in a few minutes. I need to check in at home and get Beau some water," Taylor said.

The river was shallow under the trestle. The boys were only allowed to wade in up to their knee caps. There was a current farther out into the middle of the river. It honestly was too cold to go any deeper anyway. Nobody was wearing shorts so they could only go in with their pants rolled up. The water was crystal clear today.

When the boys finally all were together again, they laughed at what had happened in the trail. "My heart's still beating fast," Bergy said. "Look what my mom gave me to share with you. It's banana bread. She made about four loaves today. It's still warm too," Taylor said. Taylor's mom was an amazing cook. She loved to bake. The boys knew to hang around Taylor's place on a Saturday because that's when she made cookies and cakes.

Kippy was two years older than Jerry but only a year older than the other two boys. He finished his yummy snack and then rolled up his pant legs and waded a few feet into the river. He could see where he was stepping and the water was only about a foot and a half deep. The boys were all wearing boots.

"Crayfish!" Kippy shouted. With that, all of the boys rolled up their pants and waded over to where Kippy was. "Right there," Kippy said as he pointed to the small crayfish. It was nearly camouflaged by colour of the small rocks in the river. Nobody wanted to pick it up because crayfish have pincers and nobody wanted to risk having a finger squished in one. "They sure look like lobsters," Kippy said. "Dad said they are small lobsters that live in fresh water, as opposed to lobsters that live in salt water," Georgy said.

"Taylor, can you get a big jar or something from your mom so we can show your dad this crayfish?" Bergy asked. Taylor ran the short distance over to his house to ask his mom. She had a large pickle jar that she gave him. "Just be careful. That's glass. Make sure you place some small rocks in the bottom and you have lots of water. Here's a plastic cup to catch him. If he pinches your finger you'll hurt for days. Also, keep the lid off so it can breathe," his mom said.

Taylor ran back to join the boys. "I found another one!" Jerry shouted. It was just a few feet from where the other one was. I saw his tail sticking out from the rocks. They sure blend in with the rocks," Jerry laughed. "This jar can hold both of them," Taylor said. Taylor told Kippy about scooping the crayfish with the cup. "That's a good idea. I tried to catch him with my hands but they can move really fast both frontwards and backwards," Kippy said.

Taylor wasted no time in putting rocks and water into the jar. He then began scooping both Crayfish into the jar. They'd take the crayfish over to Taylor's dad to show him as he'd be home from work now. They had many questions for him.

Georgy was outside sitting on the front porch when the boys arrived. "What have you boys got there?" Georgy asked. "We caught some crayfish and wondered if you knew anything about them," Taylor said. "I used to catch them in the river when I was about your age. They don't taste too bad either but you need to catch quite a few to make a meal out of them," Georgy replied. "They'll try to pinch you and they won't let go, and they can flip their tails around and hit your hands if you're not careful," Georgy said.

"These ones only grow to be about 3-4 inches long. Like the bigger lobsters, they have ten legs and two pincer claws and they eat bits of vegetation in the water called java moss. They'll also eat bits of fish, plants and insects. You can't put them in a fish tank with fish because they'll eat them," Georgy said. "People call them crawfish or crayfish. Either is acceptable. They like to hide under the rocks and are active at night. Their enemies are otters, mink, raccoons, herons and large fish. They can't survive in tap water because of the metal ions in the water, which is toxic to them," Georgy said.

"I think we'll go put them back in the river. It was pretty cool catching them. Mom told me to use a plastic cup when we were scooping them, so that we wouldn't get caught in the pincers," Taylor said.

The boys walked back over to the river and dumped out the crayfish. "Taylor, your dad really knew a lot about these crayfish," Kippy said. "Let's go look for frogs," Bergy said. "Let's see who can find the first one." Beau was splashing about in the shallow edge of the river. Taylor threw a stick in for Beau to fetch. He could play that game for hours.

Soon it was time for the boys to go home for dinner. There were no frogs to be found, which was unusual, but they talked about meeting up after dinner. Bergy said he couldn't because they were going out to his parent's friend's place for dinner. Kippy and Jerry had to stay home but invited Georgy to come to their house after he ate dinner to see the soap box car my dad is making for me. "Sounds like a plan," Taylor retorted, as he took off into his house.

Kippy and Jerry just lived up the bank behind Taylor's house. "Dad, can I please go to Kippy's place after dinner? He wants to show me the soap box car his dad has been building for him," Taylor said. "Sure son, but you must be home by seven p.m. so we can have dessert night together. Your mom made us a very special dessert for this evening," Georgy said. "What did she make dad"? Taylor asked. "A huge pineapple upside down cake. She did it for you because it's your favourite dessert," Georgy said. "Yay, she's the best mom ever," Taylor shouted. Then he scampered up to Kippy's house.

Taylor knocked on the front door. Kippy's mom answered and invited Taylor in. She handed him a cookie that she'd just finished baking. It was a jeera biscuit and Taylor loved the taste of them. He loved it when Kippy's mom baked because he was rarely there when she was making cookies. The cookies were sweet, salty, crispy, crunchy and crumbly. They were flavoured with roasted cumin seeds and smelled so good. Kippy didn't want to risk ruining his appetite for the special dessert later, but this was his favourite cookie and it was still warm.

Kippy and Jerry put their shoes on and headed out to the garage where the soap box car was. Kippy's dad was there, fitting some wheels onto the car. "Wow, does this ever look cool," Taylor said. "There's still a lot more to do Taylor. Once the wheels are on tight, I can begin to fit brakes onto the car," Kippy's dad said.

"When will you be finished? I can't wait to see the car in action," Taylor said. "Towards the end of next week. I think we'll be testing it next Saturday on the hill by your house," he said. "The steering wheel is working well with the front tires so it's just the brakes we need. We'll have to buy Kippy a helmet though first," Kippy's dad said. "I've been saving up," Kippy said. "I'll have enough when I get my allowance this week. I'm calling the car Bandit," he said proudly.

It was time for Taylor to go home for his special dessert. He loves pineapple upside down cake. His mom always loaded the top with pineapple rings, maraschino cherries, butter and brown sugar. When Taylor walked into the house, all he could smell was the sweet aroma of the cake.

"It's just out of the oven Taylor. I sent your dad to get vanilla ice cream. He'll be here in a minute. Go wash up and I'll get ready to serve it, his mom said. Talk about a treat. Life was good.

Georgy's dad arrived home and scooped the ice cream onto the cake servings. It began to melt on contact. Every bite was like a piece of heaven. "Thank your mother, Taylor. She really looks after us in loving ways and she is an amazing cook," Georgy's dad said.

"Did you know that Kippy's dad has almost finished the soapbox car for Kippy?" Taylor asked. "He put the wheels on it tonight and the steering works great. He just needs to put the brakes on it and will be testing it on the hill next Saturday. Would you like to see it dad?" Taylor asked. "Sure, why not. It wasn't too many years ago that you kids were racing your red wagons down that hill together," Georgy said. "Kippy will be racing in the 12 and under Annual Soapbox Derby in Victoria in a few months. The winner gets a new derby car," Taylor said. "Yes, that's an all-day race with the best soapbox racers from all over the province. You're chosen based on your best race time, Georgy said. Kippy's dad is a good mechanic. The car will be amazing.

Soon it was time for Taylor to get ready for bed. He was happy for Kippy but also wanted to be involved in something cool too. "Dad, do you think I can help you with the road building up on the mountain?" Taylor asked. "I'll make sure you can, probably on Saturdays. Actually, when school is out in June, you can help me at work anytime you'd like. Sleep well tonight son," Taylor said. Taylor washed, brushed his teeth and then kissed both parents goodnight. "Are you singing in church tomorrow mom?" Taylor asked. "Yes son, I am. Sweet dreams tonight. We'll have a nice breakfast tomorrow," Anna said.

SEVEN

Hide and Shriek

Georgy and Taylor loved to listen to Anna sing in church. Her voice was amazing. After church was over, it was time to eat lunch and then play outside time. The sun was shining and the other boys would be itching to play too. The banks by the railway tracks needed climbing and the forest was calling their names for a game of hide and seek.

It was still a bit chilly outside but they wouldn't be deterred from playing outside. They drew straws to see who would be the finder of the first game of hide and seek. "Taylor, are you taking Beau with you?" his mom asked. "No. He always gives us away when we're trying to hide," Taylor said. "He's going to go crazy knowing you kids are there playing," she said. "Okay, let him out. We'll use him as a finder dog," Taylor said.

The great thing about the forest was that you could hide almost anywhere but you couldn't go very far as the counter only counted to thirty. If you were fast you might be able to climb a few branches but if the dog saw you, he would lead the finder right to you. Bergy was the finder. Kippy got himself up a tree and Jerry found a great bush to hide behind.

Taylor chose a big, dead tree to hide in as the opening faced into the forest. Bergy had held Beau so that he couldn't follow the boys when they were hiding. When he finished counting to thirty, he let Beau go. "Go find 'em Beau," Bergy said. Beau took off like a shot, barking up a storm as he ran into the forest. He managed to scare a few crows away and ended up finding Gerry right away. "That's not fair," Jerry said. "I shouldn't have eaten chicken at lunch time. Beau could smell the chicken on me," he said. Bergy heard a noise above his head and looked up to see Kippy standing on a branch. He couldn't find Taylor though. Beau was running around trying to find him and Bergy scanned all the trees around him but it did no good. Taylor was well hidden. Taylor thought that if he were to start making some kind of noises, they might have a clue as to where he was.

Taylor was able to hear all of the commotion but did not dare poke his head out to look or they might see him. "Beau!" Taylor quickly called out loud. Beau's head popped up and he took off running in Taylor's direction. As the boys began to run Bergy shouted. "Hornet nest! It's a big one too," he said. That scared Taylor out of his hiding place. Now he could use it again next time because nobody saw him leave it, although the nest was hanging in the same dead tree, just on the other side from where Taylor was standing.

"We'll have to show dad asap," Taylor said. The nest was about two feet long and had to have been there for years. Thank God there were no hornets or Taylor might have been a goner. Then they moved to the other side of the tree and saw the opening in the tree. "So that's where you were hiding Taylor," Bergy said. "That's a great hiding place. You were able to get your whole body in there too," he said, "Ya, my dad showed me that dead tree a few years ago. It's funny that I'd never seen the nest before though," Taylor said. There's something to be said for looking up in the forest. Wearing hats was also a good thing so you wouldn't have a tick land on your head.

The boys rushed back to Taylor's house. "Dad, you need to see this. We found a huge hornet's nest hanging in the old hollowed out tree. I was hiding inside the tree and the boys found it high up above me on a branch," Taylor said. "Did you see any hornets?" Georgy asked. "No, but we got out of there right away. Can you please come look at it?" Taylor asked. "Sure son. Let's go," Georgy replied.

When they got to the tree Georgy was surprised to see just how big the nest really was. "It's still a bit too cold for hornets to be out yet but they would definitely come back to this hive. If you guys will help me to bring a ladder and a tree branch clipper over, I'll knock it down for you. We don't want hornets around here when it gets warmer out," Georgy said. "Okay dad. I can't wait to see this nest up close," Taylor said.

A few minutes later they arrived back at the tree. Georgy leaned the ladder against the tree and asked for two boys to stand on the bottom rung to keep the ladder from moving. Georgy climbed up about two thirds of the way and then used the tree branch cutting pole to try to nudge the nest off of the branch.

"It's really stuck on there. I'm trying not to break it. If I can free up the top part where it's attached to the tree, I bet it will fall down to you. Be ready to catch it as it won't be heavy at all," Georgy said. "As long as there's no hornets, I'll try to catch it," Kippy said. "Okay. Let's give it another go," Georgy said. He kept on nudging the top part of the nest, where it was attached to the branch until it finally gave way and fell.

"I got it!" Kippy shouted. He set it down on the ground. Thank God there's no hornets in here or I'd be toast," Kippy said. The boys waited for Georgy to climb down then gathered around the big nest. "That's huge. You should take it to school for show and tell Jerry," Georgy said. "I'd love to take it to school tomorrow Mr. Walker. Thank you," Jerry said.

"Thanks for keeping us safe dad. Can you imagine how many hornets there'd be in the nest in the summer?" Taylor asked. "They will be back. It's a good idea to keep looking up at the high branches for other nests," Georgy said. "Let's get this ladder and pole home and you kids can keep playing. Leave the nest on the porch until you're ready to go home Jerry. I'll keep Beau inside with me so it will be safe," Georgy said.

"Dad, do you have any pennies, nickels or dimes that we could have to put on the train tracks?" Taylor asked. I have a few that you boys can have. Be careful though. The engineers get worried when they see children playing around the tracks," Georgy said. "We'll hide when we hear the train coming," Taylor said. "Okay, be safe, always," Georgy said.

The boys knew that the train would be coming by at 3 pm. It was getting close to that time so they raced up onto the tracks and put the coins on the rails. They always did this near the trestle because there were bushes to hide behind as the train went by. The boys knew to put their ears to the tracks to listen for the train. They did it and were surprised to hear that it was very close by. "Hide!" Taylor yelled. They scampered behind the bushes and thirty seconds later the train came rumbling by. They saw the engineer in the window. He hadn't noticed the coins on the rails or the boys in the bushes either.

The train had passed by in under a minute. The boys raced over to look at their coins and sure enough they'd all been flattened like a pancake. They each took a coin and admired it. "Could you imagine if we derailed the engine by putting these coins on the tracks," Jerry asked. "It'll never happen. The coins are so small and thin," Kippy said.

It was time to head for home. Kippy and Jerry walked with Taylor to pick up the nest. They said goodbye to Bergy, who headed for home on the other side of the tracks. Taylor said goodbye to the other boys. "See you at school tomorrow guys," Georgy said. "I'll help carry this nest with Jerry in the morning," Kippy said.

Once inside the house, Taylor showed his mom the flattened penny. "Wow, you can hardly tell that it used to be a penny," his mom said. "You kids sure have a lot of cool and exciting things to do around here. You're so lucky to live where you live Taylor," she added.

First thing Monday morning, Georgy went to City Hall to answer any emails or phone calls that had come in over the weekend. He found an email from the surveyors who were slated to do the work on the road up to the ledge. He could now finally begin the long process to getting the work started. He had allowed three companies to bid on the surveying job, and had selected the one with the best price, who could work within the timeline provided, to be fair to all who had applied. Some of the companies had cost cutting ideas but Georgy vary on the way it needed to be built, with the hairpin turns, to keep the public safe in going up and coming down the mountain side.

It took a few weeks but city council agreed to the company awarded with the surveying work to be done on the mountain. Georgy was still working his main job as a conservation officer but kept an eye out daily on the work they were doing on the mountain. Georgy submitted a proposal on the roads name as being Ledge Lane. It was accepted.

Georgy also submitted the name Dream Mountain, with a drawing of a sign that included a dream catcher over the top part of the sign. Council approved it as well. The council members had liked the story of Georgy's dream and wished to support him.

His ideas were very good and his intentions to create something beautiful for the city were certainly there too. The drive way and viewpoint would make for a beautiful transformation on that mountain.

Georgy kept his promise and was able to hire the boys for four hours every Saturday. The job wouldn't start for a few weeks so they were still able to watch Kippy practice on the upcoming Saturday. The job would consist of picking up rocks, branches and brush etc from the proposed roadway. They'd be supplied with wheelbarrows and gloves again, just like when they worked in the trail. They'd put the refuse into piles along the road markings. They loved their jobs. Each boy talked about what they were going to do with the extra money.

"There's some heavy-duty sling shots over at Miller's Store. That would be cool if we all had those when we're in the woods," Georgy said. "My dad said that I could start saving up to buy a small rifle, and that he'd pay half. It would take a while to save up that much money but then I could learn how to target shoot," Bergy said.

"That's a good idea. You know, we could all buy a good hunting knife too. My dad could show us how to throw them," Taylor said. "Hunting knives aren't good for throwing. The throwing knives have to be balanced on each end, like the one Will made for your dad Georgy," Kippy explained. They would cost more but would be cool to own. Then your dad could show us how to throw them," Kippy said.

EIGHT

Kippy's Soap Box Car

Saturday finally came around. Kippy's dad loaded the soapbox car into his small trailer and drove it over to the hill by Taylor's place. Kippy helped his dad unload the car then put on his helmet and gloves and got into the car. Kippy's dad told him not to try doing any sharp turns to start. He wanted to see how fast it would glide down the hill. He wanted Kippy to get used to the car too, without flipping it. He also said to not use the brakes until he got to the bottom of the hill. "Remember that in the big race you'll have cars on either side of you. You need to keep the car in a straight line," his dad said. "Okay dad, I'll give it my best shot," Kippy said nervously.

Kippy said he understood. Jerry's job was to release the brake lever when it was time to begin the race, and not to push him at all. Kippy's dad was at the bottom of the hill with a timing watch. Both he and Jerry were talking on walkie talkies. Kippy's dad did the 3,2,1 countdown and Jerry pulled the brake lever.

Kippy began his descent at a quick pace. It only took 25 seconds for Kippy to fly past his dad. "Brakes!" Kippy's dad yelled as Kippy flew past him.

As Kippy took his hand off the steering wheel to apply the brakes, HIS other hand made the steering wheel turn slightly causing Kippy to veer over to the other side of the road. He stopped in time, just before crashing.

"You'll have to get use to braking suddenly, otherwise you will cause an accident," Kippy's dad said. "How did the car feel Kippy?" his dad asked. "It felt really good and solid. The wheels turn easily and it's not hard to keep it in a straight line. The brakes work well too," Kippy said. "Why did the car veer then?" his dad asked. "I took my eyes off the road to look for the brake lever. I won't do that again. I know where it is now," Kippy said.

"25 seconds Kippy. That's all it took. In the big race you'll be up on a slanted ramp so you will be flying right from the start of the race," Kippy's dad said. "You'll also be going a lot faster, right from the get go, so you need to be able to see where the other drivers are at without looking at them," his dad said.

"I'd like to try it a few more times before we try it on a steeper and longer hill. The race in Victoria will be about a minute and a half long and will have two corners in it, a left and a right. Let's get you comfortable being in the car first, then we'll take it to Victoria to practice until you're super confident," his dad said.

Kippy's next few attempts went smoothly. Kippy knew exactly where the brake lever was now and he concentrated on pulling on it the second he went past his dad. "Great job Kippy, I'm impressed!"

his dad said. "Let's go to Victoria and really test this car out," he said.

Kippy was getting so that he wanted to race against other drivers. He was in love with the car his dad built for him. He was told that there would be other kids there testing out their cars. Kippy wanted to race them all to get as much experience as possible before the big race.

NINE

Victoria Bound

The walkie talkies proved to be the answer in Victoria, since you couldn't see each other, due to the length and curves of the track. There were a few other people practicing but nobody was racing each other. They were all testing out their cars. What the parents did was share the race times with each other so that they could figure out who had the fastest car.

Kippy's dad made sure he had a good look at all of the cars there. As a mechanic, he could see how each car had been modified. There were restrictions so that the cars would be relatively the same, for fairness. Some drivers were lighter and some were heavier. That could be an advantage and allow for a better time in the pre trial races.

Each time the kids came down the hill the dads would load the cars onto their trailers and run them back up the hill. They did this a number of times. The kids were having a blast and were all feeling comfortable in their cars. Kippy had the best time over the other drivers. The dads wanted to know about Kippy's car. Kippy's dad said that lots of lube, smooth steering and smooth or next to no braking was his secret.

Kippy was becoming very confident with the car as was perfecting his cornering with each trial run. After he had done 10 runs, they packed up the car and headed for home. "Great job Kippy. You're going to do very well. We'll come back next Sunday and do it all over again," his dad said.

The boys had plenty to talk about the next week at school. Kippy said he felt confident in the soapbox car and that he just needed to be wearing goggles as the air made his eyes water and he couldn't afford to take his hands off of the steering wheel to wipe away the tears. They also had to wear gloves so it wouldn't be easy to do at all.

When Saturday rolled around, the boys had to go to work. Georgy made sure they had raincoats, gloves, hats and water bottles. He gave them a ride to the base of the mountain and showed them what he needed from them. They would work from 10-2 pm and he told them he'd be back at 2 pm to pick them up. "If I see that you've collected lots of branches and stones, I'll bring pizza and pop," Georgy said. "Yay," the boys shouted. That was motivation enough for them to get a move on.

Georgy came back at 2 pm with pizza and pop in hand. "Anyone hungry?" he shouted. The boys cheered as they ran towards the truck. "Bring the two wheelbarrows down so we can lock them in the shed," Georgy said. The boys were tired, hungry and thirsty. They'd collected a lot of debris and had a great time doing it. "Great job you guys," Georgy said. "You set to earn more money next week?" he asked. "You bet dad. That was fun. We were racing in teams of two to see who'd get the most but it was pretty even when you showed up," Taylor said.

Anna found herself getting busier and busier with her new concert booking job. The construction on the property was coming along and there was already one of three stages already built. This festival was going to be a massive event. There would be camping available for those taking in the five-day event that included bathrooms and running water. There would be first aid stations, beer gardens, water stations, ATM machines, security and garbage dumpsters. There would also be vendor tables in tents to sell souvenirs, etc. It would be totally thought out with no stone left unturned. They were looking at having traffic direction, food vendors, and hundreds of volunteers. Anna was blown away at the scope of the massive undertaking.

Anna spent her working time booking performers and bands. There was a ton of interest from local bands as well as from bands from out of town. The Headliner performances were booked by the owner of the event as there were professional contracts that would have to be put into place. All in all, it was beginning to come together. Advertising had already begun. Sponsors would be sought out and given signage and banners that would be set up around the event.

Construction on the event was scheduled to be completed a number of months later. When that was done there would be a big advertising push to sell tickets to the event. Anna worked in a small trailer down on the site. She typically worked a four hour shift each day. She was fascinated at what she was learning in the weekly meetings. "We're set to have two top performers from Nashville at the first event," Anna said. "It's starting to be the talk of the town both here and in Duncan," she said. "When the stars arrive, they will be in big busses or motorhomes. There will be a specially designed restricted area for their home on wheels to park in," she said.

The festival would supply the P.A. and other sound equipment for the three stages and there would be elevators for the technicians and musicians to use for easy access to the stages.

It would only be a matter of time before the event would be booked up and sold out. The event was taking place around a long weekend in August. The weather would be gorgeous too. Part of Anna's job was making sure all of the performers met certain criteria in order to meet the needed standards of professionalism to take part in the event.

Anna was also asked if she and Georgy would consider being chaperones in picking up performers who might be flying into Victoria. Hotel rooms would be booked for anyone needing accommodations and a shuttle service would be supplied to get them to the event.

Georgy kept juggling the road surveyors as he worked his conservation job throughout the week. When he was heading home after work each day, he would check on them. He was happy with the progress they were making and very soon they'd be able to start digging up the roadway. Georgy would also arrange for a sidewalk with guardrails to flank one side of the roadway that would extend the whole way up to the top, making the walkway inclusive for anyone wanting to walk, bike or drive up to the ledge.

Georgy knew that the road would only take about five weeks to finish and then they could begin paving and road marking. The clearing at the top near the ledge could begin. The viewpoint would offer a paved parking lot, lamp posts, a guardrail that would extend around the sidewalk along the ledge and viewpoint, a grassy area, and a large metal set of binoculars that would swivel on a stationary base, and allow people to gaze at the town below, as well as the mountains nearby. Georgy would have a bronze plaque fastened to the base for people to read about the viewpoint's existence and significance. Two benches and a water fountain would be situated near the look out too.

Georgy was getting excited. He knew that by summer time this project would be a wrap. He couldn't wait. The boys continued to work on Saturdays and were happy to be able to be saving up money. It seemed that both Georgy and Anna led hectic lifestyles but they were both contributing to their own community, and didn't mind the heavy pace. Individually, they recognised what these projects would mean to the people that lived there.

Fresh Veggies
Wild Flowers
Georgy's Roadside Stand

TEN

The Roadside Stand

It was already April. Anna was excited to be out in her garden. According to her growing calendar, she could only get lettuce in one month but in a few weeks past that she could have beets, kale, spinach, potatoes and corn. Taylor was anxious to help his mom in the garden. Broccoli, cauliflower and peas would be ready a few weeks after the corn. It was the carrots and peppers that took the longest. Two and a half months that Taylor would be watching for the carrots and peppers to appear. Then they could sell fresh produce in their roadside stand. The wild flowers would be ready by the end of June.

Georgy had asked Kippy's dad to build the stand. They agreed on a price and soon enough it was done. This was a pretty easy job for Kippy's dad. Georgy had drawn up the plans and paid for the material. When it was done, he painted it to match Georgy's house. He drew the sign on the front that said 'FRESH VEGGIES and WILD FLOWERS'. Together they moved it onto a trailer and took it over to the front of Georgy's driveway. It was a great addition to the property. Now they just needed some produce and to get the word out.

When the stand was in place, Anna, Georgy and Taylor stood looking at it. They began to discuss what they'd need, like buckets for the flowers, a small till and till tapes, etc. There were two pieces of plywood on hinges that would swing from the sides of the unit enabling the stand to be locked up at night. Georgy would buy a fridge to keep inside the unit and run a power cord from the house to keep the fridge running. "Onwards and upwards." Georgy said. "This will be exciting Anna said. We just need some veggies and we're in business," she said.

Soon enough another week of school had come and gone and the boys were set to work on the mountain again. After their four-hour shift was done, Kippy and Jerry had to scoot down to Victoria with their dad, to practice with the soapbox car again. Taylor and Bergy decided to walk along the tracks and noticed the many small round holes up high in the dirt banks, on both sides of the tracks. "Let's try to hit one of the holes with dirtballs," Bergy said. "Okay, there's tons of dirt balls," Taylor said.

It was when they started getting close to the holes, they noticed swallows leaving the holes. "Stop," Taylor said.

"They have nests in those holes. Let's see if we can climb up and see one," Taylor said. They began to climb up but about two thirds of the way up they'd slide back down. It was just too steep so they gave up on that idea.

Taylor asked if they could go for a cruise on his minibike. "Sure thing. I just have to tell my folks that I'm leaving," Bergy said. "Where do you want to go?" Bergy asked. "Let's grab our skateboards and go to the park," Taylor suggested. "I can carry the boards on the bike," he said. "Let's get everything. Gloves, knee pads and helmets, so that we don't crash and burn," Bergy said.

The skate park was only about a five-minute drive from where the boys were. Taylor loved the ride on the minibike and Bergy loved the attention. They arrived at the park a few minutes later. They were all decked out in their safety gear. Both boys were pretty good on their boards. They'd both been riding their boards since they were about four years old. They were eager to try new things that the older kids were doing. Everybody knew everybody and there was no bullying.

"Do you think your minibike will make it up the mountain side when the road gets finished?" Taylor asked. "For sure it will, but with only me on the bike," Bergy answered. "That will be in another few months," Taylor said. "The view should be really quite stunning," Taylor said. After about an hour at the park, the boys decided that they should leave for home because it was close to dinner time. They'd had a good time there and talked about how Kippy must be doing in Victoria as they made their way home.

"Thanks, Bergy," Taylor said as he hopped off the bike. "Can you manage with the skateboard, okay?" he asked. "Ya, no problem. I'll just sit on it," Bergy said. "See you tomorrow in church. Maybe we can arrange to go fishing down the trail, after church. I'll ask my dad," Georgy said. With that Bergy took off towards his house.

Taylor said hi to his folks when he got inside the house. "Did you guys have fun today son?" Georgy asked. "Yes, it's always good to practice," Taylor said. "I can't wait for Kippy and Jerry to get home so I can hear how he did today," Taylor said.

"Can Bergy and I fish for a while after church tomorrow?" Taylor asked. "You know that to catch fish, you must be up early, and done before church even starts," his dad said. That's something I'll never forget Will teaching me when I was your age," He said. "It's nothing serious. Bergy and I just want to talk and try our luck after church, for something to do. We'll take Beau with us," Taylor said. "Okay, just remember to dig up some worms before church. It's going to be sunny. Are Kippy and Jerry going too?" Georgy asked. I didn't ask them because they are in Victoria but they don't like fishing. It's not a fun thing to do," Taylor said.

The next day Taylor sat with Bergy in church. They were making plans for fishing after church. Bergy couldn't bring his minibike down to that part of the trail because it hadn't been cleared off. Georgy was going to see if Parks and Recreation would take that on so that it would be safer to walk on, Georgy did want to make it more of a public road.

After church the boys agreed to meet right after lunch. Taylor had the jar of worms and had his fishing rod ready to go.

Taylor's mom packed the boys some juice boxes, granola bars and cookies. "Make sure you don't litter boys," She said. "Put your wrappings and juice box containers into this sealable bag and bring it home. This way you won't attract any bears," she said. Bergy offered to take the worms with him since Taylor was carrying the snacks. "Have fun and don't forget to come back in time to get washed up for dinner," Georgy said.

The boys headed off towards the trail. Beau ran ahead of the boys. Taylor said that Beau would automatically start running up the trail, the wrong way, so they decided to hide on him and yell out his name. Beau came flying back down the trail and stopped near where the boys were hiding. Beau stood silent as he listened for any clues as to where the boys might be. Some pesky crows began to chatter high above them. Beau started barking at them. Taylor decided to show himself to Beau so that he wouldn't keep barking. The fish might hear him. The crows began to act in an annoying way. Pine cones began to fall so Bergy got underneath them and shouted at them to be quiet. At that moment, bird poop lander on his shoulder. "Oh no!" Bergy shrieked as he ran over to show Taylor what happened.

Taylor laughed hysterically. Bergy scraped the poop off of his coat with a small stick. He used some moss too but really needed to get water on it asap. A few minutes later, the boys found their fishing spot. It was the same spot that Georgy and Will fished at some years ago. Bergy cleaned his coat as Beau ran into the river. "Beau, you're scaring the fish! Come here and lay down," Taylor said.

They baited their hooks and cast their lines in and waited. They talked about Georgy's dream and about the work being done on the mountain side. "It will be amazing once it's done," Taylor said.

The weather began to change quickly. Taylor and Bergy had to get out of there right away. First it got cold, and the wind picked up, then it began to get dark and overcast. They needed to beat the rain. And then, a torrential downpour. The boys ran and just made it home on time. They hadn't even had a snack. "What a storm," Georgy said. "I guess you never caught any fish either," Georgy said. "Nope, and we didn't get to have a snack either. Beau was running into the river. There wouldn't be any fish hanging around," Taylor said. "I guess that's why the crows were acting all crazy like, because of the storm," Bergy said.

Taylor shared the snacks with Bergy as he made his way to his home. At least he didn't have to go far to get home. "Go get changed and we'll stay warm around the fire this evening," Georgy said. Taylor played a few games of checkers with his dad. "Do you approve of us getting slingshots with the money we're earning? There are some really good ones at Miller's Store. Or would you rather see me save up for a throwing knife dad?" Taylor asked. "I think you kids would have more fun with slingshots," Georgy said "You can get good at target practicing. A throwing knife demands skill but it's more of a serious past time that you can learn when you get older."

After dinner, Georgy built a fire. Anna brought in big mugs of hot chocolate with mini marshmallows in them. "Dad, do you remember the storm in your dream? The one that had lightning and caused a fire on the mountain?" Taylor asked. "Of course, I do. Very vividly. Lightning hit tree and he began to catch on fire. I was there on the ledge in my dream," Georgy said. The fire ended up setting the whole mountain side on fire. Thunder sounded and the faces of Spirit Chiefs became visible in the sky. "Wow, that could be a movie some day," Taylor said. "At least the book is done so others can see what happened in the dream," Georgy said.

Anna had just finished reading the book. "How exciting that must have been Georgy," Anna said. "And you were Taylor's age when you dreamt it. That's amazing," she said. "Yes, I was ten at the time. My dog Ben and I had been playing in the hot sun, over in the clover field, where you and I were married. We found some shade and laid down. I was watching an eagle circle the three on top of the ledge and fell asleep. That's when I had the dream."

Georgy, Anna and Taylor spent the next couple of hours talking about the book he had written. All the while, the wind was howling and it had become eerily dark out and rain began to pelt down on the roof. "Do you know what causes the howling sound of the wind Taylor?" Georgy asked. "Due to factors such as the surface of a tree and the air speed, one side of the wind is going to be stronger than the other when the currents rejoin. The mixing of the two currents causes vibrations in the air, which produce that ghostly howling noise that gives us the creeps. I learned that in university," Georgy said.

"That tree is still standing up there on the ledge dad. Wouldn't it be weird if there was a real fire and it burned down in real life?" Taylor said.

"That would definitely be a big coincidence," Georgy said. "I hope that day never happens." It definitely got Georgy thinking about that horrible part within his dream. Georgy began to think about what would happen if it really did happen. Would they mount a totem up there?

Soon it was time for bed. They'd managed to stay warm beside the fire all night. Taylor got ready for bed. As he hugged his mom and dad, thanking them for the nice evening, he thanked his dad for explaining the noise that the wind makes. "Now it'll never scare me again," Taylor said. "Sleep well son," his dad said. "Back to the grind again tomorrow," he said.

Georgy had a lot on his mind. "People that drive up there to the viewpoint aren't going to understand what happened in my dream," he said. "Why don't you consider providing a link for everyone to be able to access your book somehow?" Anna said. "That would help out a lot," Georgy said. "You could display a book with the link inside a glass fixture of some kind," she said. "You might also consider having the local carvers carve you a totem pole like the one in your book. That would look amazing," Anna said. "Wow, that does sound amazing," Georgy said.

Now Georgy was even more determined to make this happen. He already had a hectic workload but he knew that these new ideas just had to happen. He knew the right people to talk to and he would start designing the totem first thing in the morning. He needed to convince city council to approve getting the work done so he would start working on that too.

Georgy became so inspired at the thought of having his new era totem stand on display out on the ledge. It just had to happen. He thought he would sleep on it and begin fresh in the morning.

ELEVEN

Georgy's Dream

Georgy climbed into bed and kissed Anna goodnight. He thanked her again for her thoughts and tried to go to sleep but his mind was racing and he could not sleep. Georgy tossed and turned for hours. The wind was blowing loud and the rain wouldn't stop pounding the rooftop. Lightning cracked and gave off tremendous flashes of light in the sky. Somehow Georgy was able to get to sleep, if you can call it sleep.

(Georgy begins to dream)

Georgy found himself up on the ledge by the lone standing tree. It was totally dark and stormy out and he was cold and soaking wet. Lightning cracked throughout the blackened sky. "Why am I here and what is happening to me!" he shouted.

At that very moment the sky opened up and this time a lone Chief's face appeared through an opening in the clouds. "You still refuse to stop turning this environment into a tourist destination?" the Chief's voice said. "Must I teach you another lesson?" the voice said. "I've cared for this mountain since I was a child," Georgy said. "I want to share this paradise with others so they can see the beauty in where we live," Georgy said.

"Why can't you just leave things alone? You will destroy the mountain by digging it up and letting hundreds of people walk all over it. You put pavement all over it and destroy the natural beauty of the mountain," the voice retorted. "I have very honourable intentions in all that I do. I really do care," Georgy said. "You think you mean well but to me, your actions are deplorable," the voice shouted. "You must be shown."

Thunder bellowed as lightning cracked and lit up the sky. Then, at that moment, a bolt of lightning hit the tree beside Georgy, causing it to explode into hundreds of pieces. Georgy was forced to run. The tree was on fire. "No, not again!" Georgy shrieked.

Fire began to catch on the nearby bushes. Soon the mountain would be totally scorched. Georgy ran out on the ledge. This time, as he stared at the face in the sky, he saw the resemblance to someone he knew all to well. "Will, is that you?" Georgy shouted. "Does it matter who I am? You should have realized your mistake Braveheart. Let nature be. Leave the land alone. Let this be on your conscience for the rest of your life," the voice said.

The wind and rain picked up and drenched the flames. Georgy was flabbergasted. He looked up but the Chief's face had vanished. Georgy fell to his knees to think about what he should do. He felt like he was being shaken from the inside out.

"Georgy, please wake up," Anna said as she tried to gently shake him awake. "You're having a nightmare," she said. Georgy sat up suddenly in bed. "Oh my God Anna. I had another vivid dream about being on the ledge again. The tree was hit by lightning and it exploded with fire. I was being yelled at by another voice in the sky. When I looked at it, it was Will's face. He started the thunder and lightning. The wind and rain were unbearable.

Why did I have this nightmare?" Georgy asked. "You were reliving parts of the dream because we were talking about it for hours last night. It's in your mind," Anna said. You're also very passionate about the work you're doing on the mountain. It looks to me that this was an attempt by your own conscience to let you second guess what you are doing. I hope this dream fuels your own fire to succeed in completing the project you are committed to doing. You are a wonderful human being and your intentions are honorable Georgy," Anna said. "Get some rest now. Calm your mind and realize it was just a dream."

Morning came. Georgy woke up to Anna standing over him with a big mug of coffee. "You probably feel that you never slept at all last night Georgy, am I right?" Anna asked. "No, I can't get that dream out of my mind. It was weird that it was Will's face up in the sky. He was really angry with me. While he was alive, I respected everything he stood for. I take this as some kind of warning." "Or, is it that you are being tested to see if you will have what it takes to get this project done?" Anna said. "Whatever you do on that mountain, you do it well, and if you do get a totem carved, do it in a respectful way, with the proper permission," she said. "Absolutely. Thank you for the coffee. This is going to be a very long day for me today," Georgy said.

Georgy wasted no time in asking the elders to meet with him to discuss the carving of the totem and to have it erected on the ledge. They agreed to meet the very next day. Georgy thought to bring a copy of his book to leave with the elders so they would be better able to understand his dream and desire to get this totem done. Most people had heard of Georgy's dream but the book would help to really sell his thought process.

Georgy met with the elders and discussed his wants with them. They agreed to have a reader read the book to them in a group setting over the next few days, so that everyone could be on the same page with Georgy's wishes. They agreed to meet in another week to discuss his wishes. Georgy left to wait for their decision. He put in his resolution to City Hall. He felt more determined now to make this happen.

The following week he met with the elders. He had good luck on hie side because they had accepted his proposal. The elders felt that Georgy was honoring one of their favourite old chiefs of all time. They said that Will was loved by everyone and is still terribly missed by all. "It's really quite interesting that Will chose you to mentor. The book was an interesting read Georgy," the Chief said. "It helped us in our decision," he said.

"It will take about six months for our carvers to cut down, prep, carve and paint the totem. Then we can have it moved and erected after that," the Chief said. "This is going to be a special, out of the ordinary work of art Georgy. You called it a new era totem in your dream. We feel that we can reward you by carving it exactly the way you want it," the Chief said.

Two weeks later, at a City Hall meeting, Georgy's resolution was approved. They would allow for the additional work to be done on the ledge look out. "The plans to have these items installed look good. They will be an attractive addition to an already attractive spot on the mountain top. Thank you for your special drive to make our city more beautiful," the mayor said.

It would take six months for the totem to be finished. That would mean October. The viewpoint would be finished by mid June. Georgy came up with the idea to have the carvers work in their own secret location, and then have the totem moved up to the ledge, where they could finish the carving and painting in full view of the public, thus bringing an interest to how a totem pole is created. Georgy knew that this would encourage people to come up to the ledge to visit the viewpoint.

There began to be a lot of talk around town about what was going on up on the mountainside. Georgy was interviewed by the city newspaper and put the word out about the opening of Ledge Lane and the look out. He said the Grande Opening wouldn't happen until October but there would be a big surprise for everyone to see at that time.

People around town asked Georgy what the surprise would be but he said nothing. Even the mayor and council were asked not to say a word and to keep the secret safe. Eventually, the road, sidewalk and guard rails were completed. Now the viewpoint could be cleared and paved. It was looking really good. The workers set up the binocular stand and plaque in place. Guard rails were put up too so that you couldn't get too close to the edge. Georgy marked off the spots where the display case and totem would be erected. Benches were also set up on the ledge. Security cameras were installed too.

Work on the viewpoint continued to go as planned. Sod and flowers were brought in to help beautify the area. Street lamps and even public washrooms were set in place after the plumbing and wiring had been completed. The sidewalks, paving and painting were all that was left to do, Georgy could begin advertising the opening within the next few months.

Bergy asked Taylor if he wanted to try riding up to the top of the ledge on his minibike. "I think two of us will be okay on the minibike together," he said. "We just won't be able to go very fast," Bergy said. "We're not allowed to go there yet," Taylor said. We better go on Sunday, after church, when there are no workers around," Taylor said.

Even though there was a metal gate across the entrance, Bergy said his bike could go around it and then they could make their way around the hairpin turns and up to the top to see what was happening there. Sunday afternoon came around in no time. The boys set out for another adventure. Bergy positioned his minibike on the inside of the gate and told Taylor to hop on. "I'm glad it's not straight up," Bergy said.

The minibike handled the weight of both boys as Bergy maneuvered his way up the incline and around the hairpin corners. It only took a few minutes for them to reach the top. "Yee haw," Bergy hollered. "Wow, this is so cool up here," Taylor shouted. They parked the bike and made their way over to the edge of the ledge. They looked through the metal binoculars and were able to turn them left and right, up and down. "This is definitely a cool place to come visit," Bergy said. "I hope that security camera isn't hooked up yet or we're dead meat," Taylor said as he pointed up to the camera. "Ya, we'd better get outta here," Bergy said.

They took off back down the mountain side. When they got home, Taylor told Bergy he would tell his dad that they went up to have a look and then noticed the cameras.

"This way I won't be grounded because I told the truth. My dad always says that honesty is the best policy," Taylor said. "I just hope he doesn't tell my parents or they'll take my minibike away," Bergy said.

Taylor walked into the house and immediately called for his dad. "We're out in the hot tub. You want to join us?" his dad asked. "No thanks. I just need to tell you something. I'll be right there," Taylor said. "Bergy and I went up to the ledge to see what it looked like up there. He wanted to try the road up there before it was open to vehicles. I saw the security cameras and thought we should leave. We had just wanted to see what it looked like up there," he said.

"I'm surprised you both did that but thanks for your honesty. The cameras are live as we're watching out for vandals. I realize that people can't wait to get up there but please don't do it again," Georgy said. "Don't worry, we won't. It looked pretty cool up there. Bergy's minibike made it up there with me on the back too," Taylor said.

SOAP BOX RACING
CHAMPION
SOAP BOX
WINNER

TWELVE

Race Day

The month of June finally managed to make its way into the Walker family's lives. Anna was amazed at what their garden had produced. There were so many different vegetables ready that they needed to get the roadside stand going right away. Georgy made up some small paper flyers that the boys put on car windshields at the grocery store parking lot.

The flyer showed a picture of the stand and the $5.00 price of a mixed bag of veggies, as well as for a bunch of freshly cut wildflowers. The flowers had really grown over the past few months. Anna had her hands full digging up, washing and packaging the veggies. Georgy had arranged to cut a slot in the counter top to allow for purchases if nobody was in the stand. The money would fall into a locked box and would be retrieved when the stand would be locked up at night.

The word didn't take too long to get around. Anna found herself quite busy, especially on the weekend as people would go for drives and came by to check out the new stand. Lots of people both a bag of veggies and a bunch of wild flowers. They commented on the price being good.

Anna and Georgy replanted the garden based on what veggies would need to be grown for that time of year. Meanwhile, up behind Taylor's house, Kippy was set to race in the annual Soap Box Derby in Victoria the following weekend. Kippy's practice times were some of the best there. His dad really did know how to build a great race car. He even had a few spare wheels, in case one came off in an accident.

Kippy couldn't wait for the big race. He had a lot of confidence because he had practiced so much. He knew he had to hold the steering wheel tight and keep the car going straight, for the most part. He had learned to ease the steering as he went around the corners. He just needed to worry about other drivers hitting him and hoped he would be placed on the side of the other drivers as opposed to being in the middle of them.

There would only be four drivers competing at a time so there would be lots of races throughout the day. Only the winners from each race would continue to move forward to race again. These drivers would all be super fast with their times, like Kippy, so he knew he had to concentrate on getting ahead of the other drivers asap.

Finally, it was race day. It was early Saturday morning and the sun was shining. The sky was blue and there was no chance of rain in the forecast. The races would begin at 10 a.m. so they had to get down to Victoria to see who would go first. When they got to the location, there were people directing them as to where to unload and park their vehicles.

Georgy drove Taylor and Bergy to Victoria to cheer Kippy on. They would meet up with Jerry there. When they arrived, they found that there were sixty cars lined up in groups of four, waiting for their first race. They needed to get their race times. Georgy managed to find Kippy's dad and Jerry. There were fifteen rows of four cars lined up ready to begin the race. Kippy was in the fifth row.

The race would only take about two minutes to run. The cars started off pretty fast because they were lined up on a steep incline with a large metal brake lever that, when moved, would allow for the cars to speed down the hill at quite a clip. Kippy was placed on the outside of the four cars. He felt good about that. Georgy and the boys made their way down near the bottom to watch the cars, and to see the winners of each race. They too were excited to see Kippy in action. He had a great car and good race times.

Fifteen rows of cars meant fifteen races to start. Then the winners of each race would line up again. That's fifteen winners so there would be four more races in the second round. Out of these four races there would be four more winners. There would be one final race. The way the event was, there would be one winner, a second place, a third place and a fourth, runner up.

An announcement came over the loudspeaker. The race was about to start and to stay off the roadway. We were responsible for our own safety so we had to watch the race carefully, in case a car came directly at us. Kippy's dad joined up with Georgy and the boys near the finish line. He mentioned that Kippy had a better time than most of the other racers.

At that point the announcer called out the 3,2,1 countdown and as the starting gun sounded, the brake lever was pulled, hurling the first set of cars down the hill. As they made it to the finish line Kippy's dad remarked that the time was what Kippy's time was, but that they were starting on a steep slant that would account for a greater speed and better times. The racers times were being shown on a large electric sign. The first race showed pretty equal times but there was one racer with the best time and he was the one who crossed the finish line first.

Three more races and then it would be Kippy's turn. Each race was much like the first. No real upsets, just one winner who happened to cross the finish line first. It was now Kippy's turn. The gun sounded and soon enough Kippy was sailing past his cheering section in the lead. He won his first race and his time was fantastic. "That was so cool," Kippy shouted. He had to get out of his car because the race track employees were responsible for taking the winner's cars back up to the top of the hill. Kippy's dad had a quick look at his wheels first and asked Kippy how the steering and brakes were.

"Everything went as planned. I had no issues in the car and I got passed the other drivers right out of the gate. We get going pretty fast right from the start," Kippy said. They watched the ten other races and witnessed some of the drivers getting bumped off the race track or crashed into by other drivers who had made some driving errors. Soon enough all the races in the first heat were done. It would take a few minutes to line up the winners from the first four races. Kippy would race after the first race in the semi finals. He knew it would be a tougher race and this time he was in the middle position of the drivers. He knew he had to get a good start to be able to get away from them bumping him.

As the first race began, one of the drivers lost control of his steering going around the second turn and as he tried to correct it, lost his wheel completely, causing him to crash into the side of the road. He had been the lead car in that race too. That meant he could not be someone to worry about as he was disqualified from the race.

It was Kippy's turn to race. As the gun sounded, the four cars took off. Kippy was slightly ahead of the others and on the first turn, the car beside Kippy lost his steering and crashed into the car on the other side. That was close because if he would have hit Kippy, it would have slowed him down or sent him crashing into the side of the road. Kippy came in first again but only by a few feet. "Yee Haw," Kippy shouted again as he got out of his car.

This meant Kippy would be in the finals. Kippy's dad had watched all of the races. He saw that some of them had times that were about the same as Kippy's time. After the semi final races were done the top four racers would line up against each other for the Grande Finale race. These were the top four best drivers of the day. In the few minutes before the race was to start, the dads were looking closely at their son's cars, making sure they would function well and not cause an accident.

The announcer talked about the many sponsors of this year's race. And thanked all of the racers and their dads for their involvement and enthusiasm. He went on to thank everyone in attendance and then focused on the grand prize, the new soap box car. Everyone clapped and cheered. Then the four drivers were introduced. When Kippy's name was called the boys shouted and cheered.

As the announcer counted down to the starting gun firing, Kippy realized how nervous he was. His dad told him that the other racers would be over the top nervous too so he needed to use that as an advantage and grit his teeth for the best race of his life. This was the moment Kippy had been waiting for all year. He focused on flying out of the gate.

As the starting gun fired the racers were neck and neck. All of the cars had great lubed up wheels. Kippy could hear people cheering on the sidelines. One car began to lag a bit behind. Kippy was on the far, right side again. When they went around the first turn the three of them were together, going the same speed. By the second turn, the other outside driver began to lose control and bumped into the middle car beside him. They were racing towards the finish line. The middle car bumped into Kippy and skidded his car across the finish line. What a race!

Kippy ended up being out of control. The three cars had crashed into each other and Kippy ended up rolling his car as the car that hit him turned him sideways while he was crossing the finish line. Kippy's dad and some race track officials ran over to see if Kippy was okay. "I won dad, right?" Kippy asked. "Yes, son you did. I'm so very proud of you," his dad said. "Are you okay Kippy," his dad asked. "Yes, a lot better than this car I guess, Kippy said.

People were cheering for Kippy. He got out of his car and waved at the crowd. Kippy was deemed unhurt and was declared the winner of the race. The three drivers had just about the same race times but Kippy's car crossed the finish line first, although sideways. The other three drivers came over to congratulate Kippy. Then the dads came and shook hands. They'd all built some pretty amazing cars. They were all very proud of their sons too.

The drivers were asked to line upon a small stage beside the prize table. There were trophies, ribbons, and of course, the major prize, a new soap box car. There were a few local photographers taking pictures for their newspapers. Kippy was overjoyed. A reporter from Lake Cowichan asked what it meant to win the race. "I thank my dad for the amazing car he built me. It was the car that won the race," Kippy said.

"Winning this new car means that my younger brother can now begin to race with the car I raced today. It has a bit of damage now but my dad can repair the damage. We'll both be back to race next year," Kippy said.

After all the other racers had received their trophies and prizes, it was Kippy's turn. Kippy's dad joined him on stage. When Kippy's name was announced as this year's winner the crowd cheered. The sponsors of the race. The sponsors of the race had Kippy sit in his new car while the photographers snapped pictures of him. Then they gave him a huge trophy. Kippy was beside himself with joy.

Soon it was all over. Everyone came over to see the shiny new car and congratulate Kippy and his dad on the big win. Georgy asked if he could help bring one of the soapbox cars back with him. Georgy brought his trailer just in case Kippy won the car. That was good thinking on Georgy's part because Kippy's dad only had room for one car on his trailer. "Thanks so much Georgy. All I could think about was getting Kippy to the race on time this morning," Kippy's dad said. "You built one heck of a car. It proved to be the best," Georgy said.

Before leaving they arranged to stop and get hamburgers and milkshakes in Victoria as everyone was starving.

DREAM
MOUNTAIN
LEDGE
LANE

THIRTEEN

Ledge Lane

Now it was Georgy's turn. Absolutely everything was done. It was time to open the new road up to the top of the mountain. Georgy placed a radio and newspaper ad telling of the new road, Ledge Lane, being open the following Saturday. He made sure that the signs were up at the base of the mountain. Dream Mountain was a big wooden sign and Ledge Lane was a road sign.

Georgy lined up a reporter to be there to take photos and to interview him about the roadway and ledge look out. Georgy made sure the elders would be there as well as the Spirit Drummers to bless the mountain. The Chief told Georgy they had been very busy over the last few months making small dream catchers to hand out to everyone who attended the ceremony.

On the morning of the ceremony Georgy raced over to the bakery to pick up two large slab cakes to be given out at the ceremony. The gate wouldn't be opened until eleven a.m. but the elders were there early, setting up. Georgy met with another reporter and did another interview.

The Mayor and council were there setting up the P.A. system onto a small stage. As eleven a.m. rolled around, the gate was open and people were shuttled up to the ledge. There would be no room for cars while the ceremony was on. Volunteers were busy pouting cups of coffee and tea and handing out pieces of cake on paper plates. People were buzzing all around.

The Spirit Drummers began beating their drums and chanting. When they were done, the Mayor stepped up to the microphone and welcomed everyone to the event. He thanked the Spirit Drummers and the First Nations Band who's land the city was situated on. Then he introduced Georgy to say a few words about his creation on the mountain side.

Georgy took the microphone and asked everyone to read the plaque. He told about his dream twenty years ago and of how it was because of that dream that he knew he had to make the viewpoint possible for all to see. "What beauty we have all around us," Georgy said with a smile.

Georgy thanked City Hall for their acceptance and for allowing him to get the project done. "Please feel free to walk about and take in the beautiful scenery," Georgy said. People began to disperse and look around. They commented on the benches and pretty flowers and they took turns looking through the binoculars. They also commented on how nice the viewpoint as a whole was, and how well the parking lot and road were made. They agreed that the viewpoint was a beautiful addition to the mountain.

hAll in all, the Mayor and the citizens were impressed with Georgy's vision and accomplishments. The Mayor hinted that there was more to come and that there would be a special unveiling on the ledge in just a few short months. He said that he would be informing people closer to the time.

Georgy felt amazing. He saw the pictures in the newspapers. Kippy was also featured for his big accomplishment in winning his race. He was called the Hometown Hero Soapbox Derby Champion. He was asked to bring his new car to school to show everyone what he'd won. They put it in the gymnasium and had an assembly. Kippy felt as proud as punch.

Georgy couldn't wait until August. The garden stand had done well that there wasn't enough room to sell everything. The word had spread and they were beginning to sell two bags of veggies to people who were stopping by. Georgy and Taylor worked in the stand on Saturdays. That was their busiest day. Kippy and Jerry raced their cars but the kids always made sure to get together in the afternoon.

Everything had changed. They were all so busy now. The boys decided that every Sunday, after lunch, they would get together in the trail and just walk and talk about their week. They always took Beau for protection. They found themselves looking up high into the branches for hornet's nests too.

Georgy found out that the carvers had been working at a pretty fast clip on the totem. In another month's time they would be able to transport the totem up to the ledge to finish the carving, and allowing the public to watch the carvers work. When the totem would be ready there would be another ceremony and the totem would be unveiled and erected. Georgy would arrange to have the showcase with glass situated there on the ledge too.

(Fast forward to June.)

Both Georgy and Taylor shared something special. They shared birthdays on the same day. June 12th was their special day. It was also a Saturday and the day the totem would be moved to the ledge. "Happy birthday to us," Taylor said. "Happy birthday son," Georgy replied. "What are we doing today dad?" Taylor asked. "After we move the totem, we have to pick up a special guest that you haven't seen in a long while," Georgy hinted.

"Who dad," Taylor asked. "I can't say or it will ruin the surprise. We have to go to Duncan to pick this person up. Then, we're going to have an amazing dinner with Kippy, Jerry and Bergy," he said. "I can't wait," Taylor replied.

Taylor and Georgy made their way up to the ledge by 11 a.m. The trailer had been placed near the tree on the ledge. It had a big sign on it telling of the kind of tree it was, as well as the nation of carvers who were doing the work. The sides of the trailer folded down so people could watch the carvers at work. The trailer would be locked at night to keep it safe from vandals.

The public did come to watch the carvers. It was really cool to watch them work with such precision. The word got out that they would be there carving and painting for the next two months.

Georgy had to get moving to get to Duncan to pick up the mystery guest. Anna told the guys their gifts would be given to them right after dessert. They'd have to wait all day but it would be worth it. Anna would have dinner ready, and the other guests would be there too, awaiting their arrival. Anna had done a lot of planning for this special day.

The bus had just arrived as Georgy pulled into the bus station. Taylor scanned the people as they were getting off the bus and finally saw her. "Corky!" he shouted. "Happy birthday Taylor," she shouted back. "Happy birthday uncle Georgy," she said. Taylor made his way over to her and gave her a big hug. Corinne, Corky, was Taylor's cousin. They hadn't seen each other in about a year. "Are you staying overnight?" Taylor asked. "Yes. Your mom said I wouldn't want to miss you getting your birthday present," she said. "I don't have any idea as to what it might be, but I'm getting pretty excited now," Taylor said.

Corinne lived up the island a few hours away. She'd been given the nickname Corky when she was little. The name stuck. She didn't mind as it was only family members near and dear to her that called her that. They talked the whole way home to Lake Cowichan.

"Wow, your place looks amazing," Corky exclaimed. "A roadside garden stand too?" she asked. "And look at all these pretty wild flowers. They look so colourful and beautiful." When they got out of the car, Corky stood and admired the planter boxes filled with pansies. These are my favourite flowers," she said.

Georgy said they needed to get into the house as Anna and the boys would be waiting for them. When they got into the house they were met with a loud Happy Birthday cheer from Anna and the boys. Anna hugged Corky and quickly introduced her to the rest of the boys. Taylor asked if they could show Corky the hot tub and porch swing out by the pond. "Yes, but dinner will be on the table in five minutes," Anna said.

The boys ran outside with Corky. She loved the hot tub and fell in love with the porch swing and pond. "Taylor, I just love what you have done to your place. The garden and wild flowers look amazing and the fresh paint on the house and matching garden stand makes your place look new. I would really like to live here," she said.

"Dinner time," Georgy shouted. "Get washed up and come to the table please," he said. Anna had gone all out. There were balloons and Happy Birthday banners that she had put up in the living room. For the kids she made a big plate of yummy hamburgers with all the fixins, and for Georgy and herself she'd made a plate of baby back ribs. This was Georgy's favourite meal. For dessert she made another big pineapple upside down cake and had ice cream ready to smother on top of the cake.

The food was delicious. Then it was time for dessert. Anna lit ten candles and brought it out to set in front of Taylor. They all sang Happy Birthday to both him and Georgy. Taylor blew out the candles and then Anna went back into the kitchen and brought out an angel food cake with pink icing and sparkles. It had one candle on it, shaped like a number one. This is your favourite cake Georgy," Anna said. "Give me a second to get the ice cream," Anna said. "It looks so good," Georgy said. "You've done an amazing job Anna. Thank you," he said.

Anna asked for everyone to move into the living room to open gifts. Taylor opened his presents from Corky and the boys. Georgy went to get his camera. When Taylor had opened his gifts, and given his dad his gift, Anna said out loud. "May I please have everyone's attention! In a few minutes when I say go, I want you all to go outside to the driveway." She then made a phone call and two minutes later a truck and trailer pulled into the driveway. "You may all go out to the driveway now but stay in front of the truck please," she said.

It was Bergy's dad that had pulled in. "Hello," he said to Georgy, Anna and the kids. "What's happening?" Georgy asked. "I have a special delivery for two birthday boys," he said.

"You kids stay up front while I unload Taylor's gift," he said. "Can I help?" Georgy asked. "Nope, you're not allowed back here either," he laughed. "Here you go Taylor. This is from your mom and dad." Taylor's eyes opened wide. To his astonishment, his present was a new Keystone minibike, just like Bergy's.

"Holy crow!" Taylor shouted. "Are you kidding me? Thanks mom and dad. I love it!" he said. "We couldn't think of anything you'd much rather have and it comes with a helmet too," Georgy said. "Now we can cruise Bergy and I won't weigh you down anymore," Taylor said." Now we can take Kippy and Jerry for rides," he said. "I'll take Corky for a ride tomorrow before she has to leave," Taylor said. "I love this bike," Taylor said. "Thanks again mom and dad."

"You're up next, my dear husband," Anna said. "What?" Georgy exclaimed. Bergy's dad went back into the trailer. This time he brought out a brand-new black Harley Davidson with a big red bow on it. He started it up and said "no man should be without one of these." Georgy was speechless. The kids oogled the bikes in disbelief. Georgy looked at Anna and said "you know I've always wanted one of these?" "I love you Anna," he said.

"I love the look and the sound of this bike. "Georgy, you are thinking of yourself always putting everyone else first, before. It's high time you are rewarded for who you are and for the things that you do," Anna said. By the way, the bike comes with two helmets," Anna said. Anna reached into her vehicle and pulled out two matching black helmets. They said His and Hers in small white letters, printed on the back.

Georgy thanked Bergy's dad for his involvement in delivering the bikes. "He was the one who helped me in buying both bikes," Anna said. "Please come in for a big piece of cake and ice cream.

The kids can play for another thirty minutes and then it will be dark, Anna said.

"We'll take turns just going up the block on the mini bike, Okay?" Taylor asked. "Okay, but you must be back here in a half hour," Anna said. "Will you take me for a ride tomorrow Georgy?" Anna asked. "I'll need to get used to it first for both our safety," Georgy said. "That's a big, powerful bike," Bergy's dad said. "It's one of the greatest gifts I've ever received, next to meeting Anna," Georgy said. "How about a picnic after church tomorrow. We can feed Taylor and Corky and let them take off for their own picnic," Anna suggested.

FOURTEEN

Born to be Wild

Georgy and Taylor were two of the luckiest guys around. After church, Anna organized a picnic lunch for Taylor and Corky. It was a beautiful, sunny day. Georgy was out practicing his turns and stopping on the bike. The bike was big and heavy. Having your balance was something you needed to have because if you tipped the bike over, you might not be able to get it back upright again, by yourself. Having another person on the back is also something a driver needs to get used to as they need to be able to lean into the corners with the driver. If they don't, you could risk not making the turn and having to brake into the corner, which is not recommended to do. When he got back home, Anna asked how he felt. "It takes all of your concentration, at all times," he said. "The feeling of being out there with the wind in your face is exhilarating. It's been a few years since I last rode a bike, and I've never been on one so powerful. It takes some getting used to, for sure," Georgy said. "If you don't feel safe yet then I don't mind. We don't need any accidents. Take your time. Let me know when you're ready."

Corky borrowed Bergy's helmet. Taylor and Corky took off to see the sights. They stopped at the skate board park to show off his new bike. "That's really cool Taylor. Now you and Bergy can start your own gang," a friend said. Taylor got the nod of approval from his friends. He felt great "You want to see what my dad has been in charge of doing over the past couple of months Corky? "Yes, sure," she said. "See that mountain over there?" Taylor asked as he pointed. "That's where we're going. Right to the top. It's called Dream Mountain. That's where the ledge is. This is the mountain that my dad had the dream about, many years ago," Taylor said.

"I just got mom to order his book. I can't wait to read it," Corky replied. "This is really cool being able to go up there," she said. "Let's go. You're going to like the ride up there, as well as the view," Taylor said. When they got to the bottom of the mountain Taylor suggested that they have their picnic out on the ledge. "It's so sunny out," he said. "Look at the sharp turns Taylor. Will the mini bike be able to get us both up to the top of the mountain?" Corky asked. "Yes. Bergy and I came up here on his bike. It made it up no problem," Taylor replied. With that they started up the incline and rounded the first hairpin turn. "This is so much fun Taylor," Corky shouted. "Hold on Corky, here comes another turn," Taylor yelled.

They were up on top of the mountain within a few minutes. Taylor parked the minibike beside one of the benches by the ledge. "Are they carving a totem pole Taylor?" Corky asked. "People don't know this yet but it will be erected here on the ledge. Come read dad's plaque on the binocular stand, Taylor said. Corky read it and got a better understanding of Georgy's involvement in all of the work that was done on the ledge.

They took turns looking through the binoculars. Then it was time to eat. The carvers had just finished carving for the day. Corky got to watch a bit and she said it was cool to see them carve." Lots of people come to watch the carvers and take in the beautiful view," Taylor said. "When will it be erected Taylor," Corky asked. "I think within the next few months," he said. "My dad will put something in the newspaper to let people know the date and time," Taylor said.

"This looks amazing," Corky said. "This is a really cool thing for your town," she said. "The view is outstanding and it's a nice stroll around the ledge," she said. "I just can't wait to get his book and read about his dream adventure," Corky said. "It was a very vivid dream. Dad remembers everything," Taylor said. "It's a great read and the pictures are amazing too," he said.

"So, this is the tree out on the ledge?" Corky asked. "Yes, but I'm afraid it doesn't talk like the one in dad's book. Dad had another dream the other night. We had been talking about his dream for a few hours. When he went to bed, he had another vivid dream. It turned out to be a nightmare. He said he was out on the ledge while a terrible storm was happening. The sky opened up. There was another face that appeared in the sky. It was Will, his old friend. Will had been a Chief when he was younger. Dad said the voice was mad at him for wanting to change the mountain and caused loud thunder and lightning to strike the tree. It burst into flames and the fire began to singe the mountain side, just like his original dream.

Mom woke him up. It had been very windy and raining hard that night so I guess that was on his mind when he went to bed, Taylor said. "So, it was terrifying for him," Corky summarized. "Yes, but it also fueled his fire to continue getting this work finished. He's using this bad dream as a reminder to do a good and proper job, every step of the way. Let's take off Corky," Taylor said. They made their way down Ledge Lane. Taylor decided that he would take Corky up the trail to Will's cabin. He'd be able to try out his mini bike in the trail.

Meanwhile, Georgy and Anna had done a test drive on Georgy's big bike together and determined they would go for a drive together. Anna made up a lunch with drinks and put them in the saddle bags, along with some ice packs. They drove through Duncan to a beautiful spot called the Kinsol Trestle. The trestle is one of the tallest free-standing timber rail structures in the world. It's an old but rebuilt wooden train trestle that stands132 feet tall and 561 feet long. It's become a historical landmark and one incredible structure that is enjoyed by thousands of people year-round.

Georgy and Anna sat at a picnic table after strolling across the trestle. They enjoyed their picnic lunch together. "It's so gorgeous out here Georgy," Anna said. "It's a diamond in the rough. I'll take you to a few Farmer's Markets and let you see how popular they are around here," Georgy said. "The sky is blue and the sun is shining. It really is like living in a paradise," he said.

After a while they strolled back across the trestle and got back on the motorcycle. When they got to the first Farm Market, they saw an eight-piece marimba band playing music outside. They got a chance to watch and listen. That was really cool.

Anna was loving it. She'd never seen or heard anything quite like this and the market was buzzing with people. "What an atmosphere," Anna exclaimed.

"I have a very big surprise for you when we leave here," Georgy said. "It's not my birthday Georgy," Anna laughed. Georgy and Anna selected a few soft ice cream cups from the many home-made flavours on display inside the market. Georgy said that there was a Native Art Gallery in Duncan that he wanted Anna to see. They strolled through the market looking at everything and anything. "It's sure nice to have our big garden at home. Such healthy eating," Anna said.

After they'd finished their ice creams, they got back on the bike and scooted over to the gallery. "This should be fun. I love looking at all of this great stuff," Anna said. Georgy directed Anna over to a glass showcase that was filled with rings, bracelets and earrings. Lots of gold and silver. They were stunning to look at. The bracelets had beautiful designs etched into them. "Do you like silver or gold Anna, and of those, do you like the bangle style or wide bracelet?" Georgy asked. I like the wide bracelet in gold with the pretty design on it," Anna replied. "They are so elegant looking," she said.

Georgy asked the owner to assist Anna in trying a few bracelets on. When Anna found the right one Georgy nodded in approval and asked for it to be rung up. "Really Georgy?" Anna asked in disbelief. "Who loves you more?" Georgy asked. "And who bought me my expensive motorcycle? Believe me, it's the least that I can offer to do for you," Georgy said.

Anna was speechless. She wore the expensive bracelet home. On the way they stopped at an open market that was held in Town Square every Saturday in Duncan. There, vendors had pop up tents and tables with various stands to showcase their homemade goodies and crafts. Anna was amazed to see the quantity of local farmers who were selling their veggies. They had lots of customers buying their product. "Very interesting Georgy," Anna said. "we don't have that kind of volume to sell our veggies here. We can't seem to keep up with what our stand sells every week. They bought some fudge and a jar of Saskatoon berry jam that Georgy asked for Anna to try.

It had been a wonderful ride. "I hope Taylor and Corky have had a great time on the mini bike. They're probably still on it. I just hope he doesn't run out of gas," Georgy said.

Taylor and Corky were in the trail and within a few minutes more, were at Will's cabin. "Wow Corky said. This is where Will lived? It isn't very far from where you live Taylor. This is really cool," she said. They sat down on the bench and talked for a while. "This has been so much fun and is very interesting. Your dad really did care for Will, didn't he?" Corky asked. "Yes, he was one lucky kid. Will taught him so much. He told him stories. He really mentored my dad. When Will died he took it pretty hard but it also gave him some inner strength to keep going in everything he undertook from that point on," Taylor replied.

"Let's get back to my place Corky. We might just beat mom and dad home," Taylor said. As it turns out, they got home at the same time. Taylor had to run Bergy's helmet back to him so Corky went inside with Georgy and Anna. Beau needed to be let outside so Corky took him out and played fetch with him until Taylor got back home a few minutes later.

"Hey you kids. How'd you like to have a pizza night with leftover birthday cake and ice cream for dinner tonight'" Georgy shouted. "Yay," they both said. "We'll have a hot tub and we'll have to get Corky back to Duncan to catch the bus back home tonight," Georgy said.

So, there it was. A wonderful birthday weekend done and a visit from Taylor's favourite cousin. Corky stared at Anna's bracelet. "That's so beautiful," Corky said. "Thank you Corky. I feel blessed to have it. "You deserve it mom," Taylor said. "We shouldn't ever forget just how much we are all blessed," Anna said. "I think at times we take it all for granted, she said.

They had dinner and a quick hot tub. "It was so nice of you to come and visit us Corky," Georgy said. "What a blast!" Corky replied. "Those were some birthday presents too," she said. "I have a set of earrings that I'd like to give to you Corky," Anna said. She went to her bedroom and got a small pair of silver hands earrings that were clasped together. "Believe in something so that you won't fall for anything," Anna said. "They're so pretty. Thank you," Corky said.

They left for Duncan. When they pulled into the bus station Corky thanked them all for their generosity. They all got out and hugged each other goodbye. "Thanks for being a part of my dad and my birthday Corky," Taylor said. Corky blew him a kiss and boarded the bus. As Georgy left for home he said to Anna. "I wonder what this week will bring?" he asked jokingly. This was one wild and memorable weekend," he said.

FIFTEEN

Eagles Again

The roadside stand had been a big hit in town. Anna had taken that on and had stayed pretty busy with it. The auto watering system had been a blessing by keeping the whole garden watered. Anna had to pull back from singing away from town and was becoming really comfortable with her family life. She never forgot the about the African marimba music that she'd heard at the market. She eventually looked into taking lessons and was signed up in no time, for a lesson on Wednesday afternoons that would run for two months.

Anna rented a unit from the instructor so that she could practice. Georgy and Taylor liked the sound of the marimba and were looking forward to the beginner's recital that would happen in two month's time. Anna continued to sing in her rotation at church. She was a beautiful singer.

The carvers were making good ground on the totem pole and the talk around town was that everyone was happy with the improvements that were made on the mountain.

When Georgy got home from work, Taylor greeted him. "Look up at the ledge dad. Do you see what I see?" Taylor asked. Georgy looked up and saw two eagles circling above the lone standing tree out on the ledge. "You've got to be kidding me. Eagles again, after all of these years. To me, it's a sign. They left after Will died. They used to nest in that tree. We'll have to take a closer look next time we're up there," Georgy said. "I'm thrilled. It's just like the dream Taylor," Georgy said with a smile. "Can we go on Saturday?" Taylor asked. "Sure. You know, one eagle flying is cool, but two can only mean one thing, and that's offspring," Georgy said.

When Saturday rolled around, Georgy, Anna and Taylor took a drive up to the ledge. To their amazement they saw the nest, way up in the tree. There was only one eagle flying around so that meant the other one was in the nest.

"I asked my teacher and he said that the babies would hatch in ten to twelve weeks," Taylor said. "This is exciting. I've only seen an eagle once and now we're going to be living close to a family of eagles," Anna said with a grin. The babies will be trying to fly at around the sixteen to eighteen-week mark. How cool will that be?" Taylor asked.

"They have to make it through the first winter," Georgy said. "Over 70% of young eagles die during that time. At least our winters tend to be on the mild side here," Georgy said.

"Let's go get some groceries so that we can get back out on our bikes," Georgy said. "Yahoo," Taylor answered. They bought what they needed and then scooted over to Miller's Store for an ice cream cone. "It's a good thing we remembered to buy Beau some dog treats. This way we all get a treat," Taylor said.

When they got home, Taylor took Beau outside and gave him a treat. Georgy and Anna put the groceries away. The sun was shining and it was warm outside. Anna decided that she should open the roadside stand as she had lots of bagged up veggies she needed to sell. "I'll sit there and read for a while. Maybe I'll take the marimba over and practice between customers," she said. "I'll spell you off when I get back from a quick ride," Georgy said.

Taylor had decided to play with Kippy and Jerry because they offered to teach Taylor how to drive the soap box car. They were going to be racing on the hill that afternoon. Just then Bergy showed up on his mini bike.

"Hi Bergy," Taylor said. "You want to learn how to drive a soapbox car? Kippy said he'd teach me if I let him ride my mini bike," he said. "Ya, sure," Bergy said. They rode up to Kippy's place only to find the soapbox damaged and missing a front wheel. "That doesn't look good," Taylor said. Kippy's mom came out and said that Jerry had crashed the car and had broken his wrist. He had been taken to the hospital. "Oh no," Bergy said. "What happened to cause the accident?" Taylor asked. "The boys were racing down the hill. They scared a small dog that happened to be walking on the side of the hill. It ran across the road, right in front of the boys. Kippy swerved to miss the dog and side swiped Jerry causing him to hit the gravel on the side of the road. Then his car slid and crashed into the only pole on the hill. He snapped his wrist on the steering wheel when he hit the pole," she said. "Kippy went with his dad to be with Jerry. They've been gone about an hour now so they hopefully will be coming back soon," she said.

"Please tell Jerry we're sorry. Who owned the dog?" Taylor asked. They didn't know. They hadn't ever seen it before. It must be a stray," Kippy's mom said. "You boys stay safe," Kippy's mom said. "We will," Taylor said.

The boys took off. "Let's go to the skateboard park Georgy. We can watch to see if Jerry is going to drive by," Taylor said. When they got there Taylor told Bergy that his dad had cautioned him on swerving to hit an animal because it might make him veer into an oncoming car and become seriously injured. "Wow, I wouldn't have thought about that. That's good to know Taylor," Bergy said.

About twenty minutes later, Kippy's dad drove by and honked at the boys. The boys flagged him down. Jerry rolled down his window and showed the boys his cast. "Holy!" Taylor said. "How long will you have the cast on for Bergy?" Bergy asked. "Six to eight weeks," Jerry said. "A stupid dog cut me off and I hit Jerry in a race," Kippy said. "We were neck in neck too," Jerry said. "Now dad has to try to fix the damage. The dog took off running. I've never seen it around here before," Kippy said.

"Well, your cast looks cool. You'll be popular in school on Monday," Taylor said. "It hurts pretty good. It's going to be weird only having one hand," Jerry said. We better go and show mom.

See you guys tomorrow," Jerry said. As they went home, Taylor and Georgy talked about all the things that Jerry was going to have a hard time doing with one hand.

When Taylor got home, he found his dad sitting in the roadside stand. "How's it going son?" Georgy asked. Taylor told his dad what happened to Jerry. "He'll be a one-armed bandit for a few months then," Georgy said. "Ya, it won't be easy using only one hand, and it's his right hand that is broken," Taylor said.

"Where did you ride today?" Taylor asked. "I cruised the highway and went into Duncan and back. It was about a 45-minute drive. Just a quick one to feel the on my face," Georgy replied. "How has the stand been today?" "Pretty good. People have been asking for cookies and loaves of cheese bread. I know your mom loved the idea because she's in the kitchen baking chocolate chip and peanut butter cookies as we speak," Georgy said. "This is turning out to be a fun hobby," Georgy said.

"I'm about to shut down this stand and lock it up son. You want to have a ride on my Harley before dinner?" Georgy asked. "Yes please," Taylor replied. Taylor and his dad walked in to tell Anna what they were up to. The smell of cookies filled the air inside the house. "Those smell so good mom. Can we have one," Taylor asked. "Just one each. Don't be late for dinner. We're having meatloaf with garlic smashed potatoes," she said.

Georgy decided to take another run into Duncan. The ride lasted about 45 minutes. When they got back home, Taylor was beside himself. "I can't believe the power this bike has," Taylor exclaimed. "It gets cold even on a warm afternoon when we get going fast. That's why a person needs a good coat and gloves," Georgy said.

They went inside and washed up for dinner. "Now that school's out, what are you going to do with yourself all summer Taylor?" his mom asked. "Can I rely on you to do some garden chores and work in the roadside stand to help me?" she asked. "Sure mom. About how long each day cause Bergy and I want to get paper routes. They'd need to be delivered twice a week," Taylor said.

"For the most part, the stand can run itself. It's really an honour system with people paying money. We installed cameras to watch for any theft though," Georgy said. "Okay mom, I think that should work out." Taylor said. "Your allowance will get bigger and you'll be able to enjoy a few delicious cookies while in the stand too," his mom said. "As long as I have lots of change. The bags are $6.00 each and people give me tens and twenties all the time, "Taylor complained.

Anna served up the meatloaf, mashed potatoes and a nice garden salad. "Don't forget that we have a walkie talkie in the stand if you need any help Taylor," Anna said. Georgy gave thanks for the wonderful food they were about to eat. "This salad is the result of the fruits of our labor," he said. "I'm so very proud of you both," Anna said. "And we're so very proud of you too Anna," Georgy said. "Can I rely on you two to clean up the dishes? I need to package up and start freezing these cookies. I think they're going to be a big hit," Anna said. "As for the loaves of bread, I think I will bake some large cheese bread loaves and maybe some garlic bread tomorrow," she said. Something tells me that we're about to get a lot busier with our stand," Anna said. "Word has it that people enjoy coming here to pick up their veggies. It won't take long for the word to get out that we're selling baked goods too. It'll be a big hit, you watch," Georgy said.

SIXTEEN

Erecting the Totem

Georgy kept in touch with the elders. They were practically finished the carving and would still need another few weeks to have it painted. Georgy set the date for the ceremony as being August 20th, a special day for Georgy. That was the day he first met Anna and was also the date in which they were married.

Georgy had an amazing idea. He would have an eagle cam set up near the nest so that people could watch the hatching of the eaglets. City Council thought it was an amazing idea and gave approval to get the camera set up, after the totem pole would be erected. They would need the height of the pole to put the camera on.

Georgy found himself with only two weeks to go before the ceremony. Just like the last time, the Mayor would speak, the Spirit Drummers would drum and chant, and the Elder Chief would speak to bless the event. Georgy knew that he too would be expected to say a few words too so he'd prepare for that.

The hole was dugout in preparation for the totem pole. Another smaller, rectangle hole was dug out for Georgy's cement structure.

Georgy had the stage and P.A. system booked and he enlisted the help of businesses in town to supply the snacks and beverages. There would be balloons and of course, the media would be there to cover the long-awaited event.

Georgy's book had begun to be noticed. He had already received positive reviews on it. Nearly everyone in town knew of his dream and knew now of the significance of the work he had organized on the mountain. There would be a lot of people up there to watch the totem being erected.

When the day came, it was beautiful out. Everything was ready and the Spirit Drummers were set to begin. Shuttle were arranged to get people up and down the mountain side again. They started to arrive.

At 11 a.m. the Mayor welcomed everyone to Dream Mountain. He thanked the local Band for the land the city was built upon and asked for the Spirit Drummers to bless the ceremony with their traditional drumming and chanting.

When they had finished the Mayor called upon the Chief to say a few words about what the changes to the mountain meant to his people. The Chief began in saying that the way in which City Hall and Georgy had handled the work being done to the mountain was both respectful and proper. He talked about the dream Georgy had as a younger boy some twenty years earlier and he talked about Will and the mentoring relationship he had with

Georgy and told of the name Braveheart that was given to him by Will for his ability to listen, learn and adapt.

The Chief went on to say that the totem that had been carved was in fact a new era totem, just as Georgy had imagined in his dream years ago. "Thank God the tree is still alive. Georgy Walker is about to tell you why," he said. He passed the microphone to Georgy.

"This is the tree that I looked up to as I lay in the clover field Twenty years ago. I used to watch an eagle flying high above this lone tree on the ledge. When Will died the eagle left and didn't return until June, when the work on the ledge was done. Now there are two eagles but only one circles the tree. That means that the other is nesting. In another 10-12 weeks their offspring will hatch. I have arranged with City Hall to have a non evasive, low light to be set up near the nest so that we all can watch the eaglets hatch. The live streaming will be ready soon.

Right now, I am pleased to say that the carvers did an amazing job in recreating the totem that I had from my dream. I have a small cement unit with a glass top that will allow people to see the book relating to my dream, as well as a link to where they can look it up online. For now though, I think it's time to stand this totem pole upright," Georgy said. Georgy gave the thumbs up, okay to go sign to the Chief.

The Chief shouted to the men to begin lifting the totem off of the trailer. They used a small crane with ropes and straps. The totem was lifted over the hole and was lowered down slowly so the men could direct the base of the totem into the hole. When it was upright the men pushed big rocks, gravel and dirt around the pole to keep it steady. They also dumped cement in and around the gravel and dirt to hold the totem in place.

When it was done everybody clapped and cheered. Anna hugged Georgy because his dream had finally become a reality. He'd done so much for the town he lived in. Georgy thanked the local First Nations people, the carvers and the Chief for allowing this to happen on the mountain.

He thanked the Spirit Drummers, the Mayor and Council, the people in attendance and the stores that had donated food towards the ceremony. "I feel blessed today," Georgy said.

Georgy explained the characters on the totem. He wanted everybody to understand the meaning behind each character. Will, Georgy, Eagle, and the round hole in the top. "This took a few decades to come to fruition, but I believed in my heart that it could be done. Thank you all for your kindness. You now share in my dream," he said.

"Georgy," the Mayor interrupted. We at City Hall wanted to honor you so we have attached a lifetime achievement award in the form of a bronze plaque. It's the same as the one you had on the totem in your dream. I'll read it out loud. It says..

You had it in your heart, you kept an open mind, you spoke in sound advice, you cared to help mankind. From the citizens of Lake Cowichan."

Georgy hugged the Mayor as the crowd clapped in sincere appreciation. "I'll never forget this day," Georgy said smiling. Georgy thanked and dismissed the crowd and invited the reporters to come and ask their questions.

After everyone had left, Georgy went home to relax with his family. "What a day!" Georgy said. "What a year!" Anna said. "The gate will be shut in the evening to prevent people from going up to the ledge. The eagle cam will be installed in the morning," Georgy said.

"Why don't we go sit by the pond and sip on a glass of wine Georgy," Anna asked. "That would be nice," Georgy said. "The cushions on the swing are large and really soft but what if I fell asleep?" Georgy asked. "I'd let you nap until dinner time and then come wake you up, "Anna said. "I don't want you to have to cook dinner tonight Anna. Let's go for Chinese food to celebrate," Georgy said. "Okay, but first, let's get you down to that porch swing. We need to reflect on the past year," Anna said.

Georgy talked with Anna about being happy to just focus on his regular job as a conservation officer again. "Maybe you'll find time to join up with the marimba band with me," Anna said. "It's too much like work Anna," Georgy said with a laugh. "Besides,

I'd much rather watch and encourage you with your music and singing," Georgy said.

I guess the development for the outdoor rock concert is nearly finished too. That'll be one wild and amazing long weekend to remember," Georgy said. "We'll soon see Georgy. We're having another staff meeting next week. I'll know more then," Anna answered. In the meantime, I can't wait to see your smiling face in the newspaper this coming week," Anna said. The ceremony, your totem and the eagles will be the talk of the town for a very long time," she said.

SEVENTEEN

A day at a time

Everyone loved watching the video stream of the eagles in the nest. The two eaglets hatched and it was the most incredible sight to see. The pictures made front page news. They were definitely a nice addition to the now famous ledge. City Hall said they would leave the video streaming available until such times as the eagles had left the nest. That was nice as people enjoyed watching them. It's not something you see every day.

Bergy and Taylor would continue to ride their mini bikes around anywhere and everywhere. Kippy and Jerry were both certain to become soapbox derby champions and Corky would be pleading her case to come stay with her cousin for the next summer vacation. Lake Cowichan was a cool place to be. As for Beau, he was one lucky dog to belong to the family that he did.

Georgy would soon be taking Beau to work with him everyday for protection in the bush. Georgy and Anna would continue to do what they do best. That is to help make a difference in someone's life everyday.

END